TARZAN

THE JUNGLE WARRIOR

Andy Briggs

faber and faber

First published in this edition in 2012
by Faber and Faber Limited
Bloomsbury House,
74–77 Great Russell Street,
London WC1B 3DA

Typeset by Faber and Faber Ltd

Printed and bound by CPI (UK) Ltd, Croydon, CR0 4YY

A CIP record for this book
is available from the British Library

ISBN 978–0–571–27353–9

For Mum – a jungle queen!

Ataro Okeke was a mass murderer, although you wouldn't know it by looking at him. The short, stocky bald man was wreathed in cigar fumes as he stood on the balcony of his luxury apartment gazing across the night-time urban sprawl of Kampala's Nakasero Hill, which was now covered in skyscrapers and construction cranes – the mark of progress. It had changed dramatically in recent years. He could remember when everything he saw lay under a cloud of war with Tanzania. But that was when he was just a child.

Inside, the telephone rang. Okeke sucked on his cigar as he opened the wide French windows and entered the air-conditioned apartment. A pair of zebra pelts hung on the wall, one on either side of the doors. The entire apartment was a gallery of dead wildlife – from the polar-bearskin rug to the ivory elephant tusks that perfectly framed the dining room door — a testament to the many animals he'd slaughtered.

Okeke stubbed out the cigar in a bowl crafted from a tortoise shell and picked up the phone.

'Yes?' He listened to the voice on the other end of the line. It was his agent. The middleman not only served as a convenient buffer between him and his clients, who demanded exotic animals, but he was also a pawn, an easy scapegoat who allowed him to stay beyond the reach of the law. Okeke felt he was untouchable.

'That's a very specific request he has. That will cost him $300,000 minimum. They're critically endangered.'

While Okeke waited for his agent to relay the information to the buyer, his gaze lingered on an ornamental gorilla skull mounted in a display case on his desk. It was a huge specimen, one he had hunted himself. After a short time his agent returned with a brief acknowledgement that the deal was on, and the line fell dead.

Okeke dialled another number. As it rang he opened the glass case and ran his fingers across the skull. The call was answered on the fifth ring. The voice was low, a whisper made all the more harsh by its pronounced Russian accent.

'You're a fool calling me now! You could have blown everything.'

Okeke smiled. He enjoyed annoying the Russian, although he was careful never to go too far. As much as Okeke hated to admit it, the Russian was his most valuable asset.

'I have another task for you.'

'I'm busy.'

'This one you'll like. I assure you.'

★

Across the border to the east, in the vast Kenyan savannahs, the Russian lay flat on the ground, lit only by the partial moon and concealed by tall, slender grass. An earpiece relayed Okeke's message and, despite himself, he couldn't help smiling.

'I have a particular interest in that region,' the Russian replied. 'The White Ape legend . . . I'll be in touch to discuss my fee.'

He abruptly hung up and gazed through the nightvision scope attached to the top of his Saiga semiautomatic hunting rifle. The 30.06-calibre bullets were so powerful they could bring down an elephant. Which was exactly what he was planning on doing.

The bull elephant was grazing on an acacia tree, its slender trunk plucking the tastiest leaves from the top branches. The hunter guessed it was about forty-five years old, judging by the impressive set of tusks it sported.

Just a little older than I am, he thought. *Time to retire.*

His finger hovered over the hair trigger as he centred the crosshairs on the middle of the animal's skull. He held his breath, not out of anticipation but to eliminate any tiny movements that could throw his shot wide. Even if he was armed to the teeth he didn't want to risk facing a charging elephant.

The high-velocity round cracked across the landscape and the elephant fell with a thud. The Russian leaped to his feet, and as he did so the foliage behind him came alive as his entourage burst out of their concealment carrying the tools to finish the job. The men knew exactly what they had to do. They moved with speed and precision, wearing night-vision goggles to guide them. They never used torches, which would easily give their position away.

The Russian pulled his own night-vision goggles down from his forehead and the world immediately lit up in grey-green hues, just as he had seen through the night scope. With the goggles on, he looked like an insect stalking through the grass. He approached the elephant and saw that its chest was still heaving even though its skull had been cleaved open. The ground was awash with blood, and he was careful not to get too close. Blood was difficult to wash off his favourite boots.

He pulled back the rifle's bolt, chambering another round. He didn't need the night scope to aim at the elephant's heart. Another shot echoed across the savannah, scaring away any scavengers that may already have smelled the blood.

'OK, hurry. I don't want to be here when the patrols turn up.' On many occasions he had come under fire from anti-poaching patrols, especially in Kenya where they were exceptionally vigilant and well armed. He had no qualms about firing back. He'd lost count of the men he had injured and even killed on patrol. He didn't enjoy it; there was no sense of sport in shooting men. It wasn't the same as pitting his wits against the cunning of a wild beast.

That was sport.

A chainsaw revved in the darkness and came down on one of the tusks, chewing effortlessly through it. The Russian wished there was an easier way of transporting the elephant carcass; he could get a good price for the various parts. Somebody somewhere would be convinced that an elephant liver was a cure for cancer or some other nonsense. Instead, they would just take the ivory and leave the body to feed the vultures and hyenas.

'The circle of life,' he said to himself sarcastically.

A small ferrety man looked up as he helped pull the first tusk free. 'Instead of muttering, you could come and get your hands dirty,' he grumbled. Paulvitch was a Russian too; the others were Kenyans desperate for cash. They were easily recruited and easily expendable, whereas Paulvitch was an old friend. He was the only man alive whom the Russian allowed to speak to him in such a familiar way.

'I did the hard part,' he reminded Paulvitch. It was true. He had been tracking the elephant for several days, following the signs, closing the distance on the animal. For two hours he had crawled through grass just to get close enough. 'So shut your mouth, *drook*. And hurry up. We've got a far more interesting job lined up now.'

'Where to next?'

The Russian pulled off his night-vision goggles and gazed across the moonlit grassland. He scratched his goatee beard and turned his thin, cruel face upwards. His black eyes narrowed in anticipation. His mind was already racing with the possibilities of the next assignment. This one could test his hunting craft to its limits. He relished the task ahead. He was Nikolas Rokoff, the greatest hunter in the world, but it had been a long time since he'd had a real challenge. This might be just what he needed.

'The old Congo. We've got a gorilla to catch.'

2

Robbie Canler drove the supply jeep into the camp and sighed when he saw Jane Porter was the only person around. She glanced at him, then quickly looked back at the book she was reading. He climbed from the vehicle and glanced around Karibu Mji, the adopted name of the logging camp that Jane's father had established deep in the Congo jungle. The operation had recently been moved even further into the humid rainforest away from the mountain Karibu Mji, dismantled and rebuilt to provide extra protection from the dangers of the jungle – but the name had stuck.

'Have you seen Clark anywhere?' asked Robbie as he combed his fingers through his tangle of black hair that the wind had messed up. The jeep had no air conditioning so he had to drive it with the windows down, even during downpours.

Jane's eyes never left the page. 'No.'

7

Robbie was about to ask another question but instead headed towards the camp's office. If Jane wasn't in the mood to talk to him, he wouldn't force the issue.

★

Jane watched him walk away out of the corner of her eye. The last few weeks had been difficult to say the least. Their run-in with a gang of jungle rebels had made them all face the difficult choice between staying in the jungle or closing up camp for ever.

A month before, Jane would have been cheered by the news that they might be going back to the States, but now she faced a dilemma. Suddenly she had no wish to leave the jungle, yet if they stayed, now more than ever she was opposed to how her father, Archie, was plundering it.

In the end Archie's business partner, Clark, had persuaded him to carry on. Jane had known Clark all her life and knew that the one thing he prized above all else was money. It hadn't taken him long, behind closed doors, to talk her father round.

New equipment had been brought in, at a huge cost to the operation. Another expense Archie had insisted on was a set of satellite phones for himself, Clark, Robbie and Jane, so they could stay in touch no matter where they were. All they needed was a clear patch of sky.

Ever since they had made the decision to stay, a strange mood had descended on the camp. Jane found herself being left out of conversations and odd glances were cast her way when people thought she wasn't looking. Even Robbie was dealing with her at arm's length. Things just weren't the same between them since Robbie had confided that he was wanted for attempted murder. He revealed how his sister, Sophie, had died a victim of their abusive stepfather. On finding his sister's cold, frail body, Robbie had clubbed his stepfather across the head. Then, convinced he'd killed the man, had fled his hated home and left the country as quickly as possible, a burden of guilt weighing heavily on his shoulders. He stowed away on a cargo ship until Clark had found him.

After a little Internet digging, Jane had uncovered the fact that his stepfather was not dead. She'd thought Robbie would be pleased with the news and that it would ease the guilt he felt; instead, her announcement had made him sullen and thoughtful. Several times she tried to talk to him about it, but each time he changed the subject. Once, he was so desperate to avoid that conversation that he pointed to the camp's jeep and said, 'Do you want me to teach you how to drive?'

The message was clear – his past was no longer up for discussion. Jane felt hurt; she was only trying to help. But those feelings were quickly overshadowed when Robbie showed a sudden interest in Tarzan.

'Maybe we should go and pay him a visit?' he had suggested during one driving lesson. 'Check he's OK.'

At first, no one believed Jane's tales of meeting the mysterious 'white ape', or *Negoogunogumbar* the evil spirit the locals all feared – a man who had been raised by wild apes. It wasn't until Tarzan had rescued the loggers from Tafari and the hands of the other jungle rebels that they finally accepted he was a living, breathing man. Not just a man, according to details Jane had uncovered through her Internet research – Tarzan was an English aristocrat, the rightful Lord Greystoke and heir to a vast fortune.

Now Clark and Robbie were suddenly showing more of an interest in Tarzan, it was easy for Jane to see the spark of greed that burned in Clark's eyes and she ignored their requests to be introduced to him properly. Even if she'd wanted to, she couldn't. She hadn't seen Tarzan since he'd led them all back to the old Karibu Mji camp and then vanished into the jungle.

Jane kept a constant eye on the trees for any sign of him. Even though he hadn't shown himself, she was convinced he was out there. Watching.

★

Inside the camp office, Robbie drank a pint of cold water in one go. He was parched after the long drive from Sango, the nearest supply town. The camp's new location was far from any government taskforces patrolling the area, but it meant an almost six-hour drive along punishing rocky roads that were no wider than animal trails.

'Did you get it?' Clark asked impatiently.

Robbie pulled a crumpled brown envelope from his safari jacket and tossed it onto the desk. Clark opened it and eagerly extracted the papers from inside. They were printouts of various websites, all faded and poor quality.

'Not bad, not bad at all, mate,' said Clark, reading through. He pointed to the figures on one page. 'Is this right?'

Robbie shrugged. 'As far as I can tell.'

Clark gave a low whistle. 'That's a lot of cash.'

Robbie nodded absently. He'd spent the best part of two hours trawling through the Internet, gathering any information he could on the Greystokes. He knew Jane had done the same, but Clark had explicitly told him not to involve her.

'There were no emails from them,' Robbie added.

Clark put the papers down and stared thoughtfully out of the window. 'They're not going to believe us without solid proof.'

Clark had contacted the family the moment Jane had revealed the ape-man was their long-lost heir and worth a fortune. Clark was counting on the family offering a substantial reward that would set him and Robbie up for life.

'I don't know why we don't let Archie in on this. He'll get Jane to tell us more,' urged Robbie

Clark laughed as he carefully folded the printouts back into the envelope. 'Oh, no. Not that we won't cut him in on the reward,' he quickly added. 'But tellin' him now ain't right. Firstly, that girl's got her dad wrapped around her finger. Arch still feels guilty after what happened. Secondly, you know what he's like.'

Robbie studied Clark. He was South African and in his forties, although he acted like a man half his age. Robbie owed Clark everything and this new opportunity was giving him the chance to make a very real fortune – more than he could ever earn logging rare hardwoods. With it he could finally be free of his past and start a new life. But that didn't mean he approved of the way Clark was exploiting Jane's friendship with Tarzan.

'He would tell Jane everything we've been planning,' Robbie said quietly.

'Exactly!'

'What's so bad about that?' Robbie hated going behind Jane's back.

Clark gave him a hard stare. 'We don't want her to go and scare our boy off, do we? After all we're doin' what she wanted. Wasn't she the one thinkin' it best we reunite him with his family? Not my fault she had a change of heart. We're helpin' him find out about his past.'

Robbie felt his cheeks burn, even though he was certain Clark hadn't intentionally directed the last comment at him. Jane had let slip that he thought he'd killed his stepfather, but after realising her mistake, she convinced everybody it had been a simple accident back in New York, not anything more sinister. He assumed nobody knew anything further and he hoped Jane would keep it that way – yet paranoia crept over him and he couldn't stop the words tumbling from his mouth.

'What's so good about that?'

He tried to avoid eye contact but he could see Clark looking at him oddly and, not for the first time, Robbie wondered how much more Clark knew about his past.

'Some of us may be runnin' from our past. But some blokes, like our friend Tarzan, just need a little help to stop runnin'.' Clark gave a lengthy pause, then added, 'Don't ya think?'

Robbie changed the subject. 'I think we're not going to get much further than the contents of that envelope without a little more help.' He glanced out of the window and noticed how dark it was getting. 'I'd better unload the supplies off the jeep.'

He'd made it to the door when Clark called out in a low voice, 'Proof, mate. That's all we need, not help. Proof that Tarzan really is the rightful Lord Greystoke. Proof that there really is a crashed plane out there –' he waved a finger towards the jungle – 'and that his family was on when they went missin'.'

Robbie nodded, then quickly left the cabin and walked over to the jeep. Already the sun was hovering close to the tree line, casting ruby-red light across the clouds. The loggers were returning from their explorations; chainsaws and machetes slung across shoulders. Robbie waved a silent greeting to each of them, knowing they'd be too exhausted to engage in conversation. They headed to the bar where the camp's cook, caretaker and part-time teacher, Esmée, had a stew going. Robbie's stomach rumbled as he caught the delicious aroma.

At the jeep, he pulled the loading straps free and heaved a pair of rice sacks onto his shoulder. He trekked towards the bar and saw Jane was still outside, book in hand but her attention on the trees. He knew she was hoping Tarzan would appear. Although she'd often told him about the derelict aircraft hidden in the jungle, the place where Tarzan and his ape family lived, she had never once offered to take him there. Robbie sighed; if he could locate it then he'd have concrete proof that the Earl of Greystoke had been found.

Then the reward would be theirs, all his problems would disappear and he could at last turn his back on the jungle for good.

A cool breeze gusted between the mighty mountain peaks, hauling in heavier rain clouds. The rain drummed on the fuselage of the aircraft lying on the edge of a broad plateau. Over the years, vegetation had clung to the plane, camouflaging it from prying eyes. One wing had been torn off against the mountain, the other stretched over the cliff. Ordinarily the cliff top offered an unparalleled view across a lake, but today it was smothered in cloud.

Several gorillas sheltered by broad tree trunks and leafy canopies around the plane. They watched the weather cleanse the mountain as they waited patiently for the storm to pass.

Tarzan, however, shifted restlessly as he waited for the rain to stop. A large hole in the fuselage formed an artificial cave. It was there he took refuge, and without the long, thick fur the gorillas possessed, he shivered. A young ape rolled carefree at his feet.

Karnath, orphaned by the rebel Tafari, now kept as close to Tarzan as possible, even though a kindly female gorilla had adopted him as her own. Karnath jumped as lightning flickered across the sky. Tarzan gave a series of throaty grunts to assure him everything was OK and the gorilla continued playing, bouncing across the ageing aircraft seats, even when the thunder shook the mountain.

Tarzan envied Karnath. He wished he could just ignore the problems of his *mangani* family. Not only were they grieving for their lost family members after Tafari's attack, but they were also dangerously low on food. The *mangani* had spent too long in the immediate area. Now choice shoots and bark were at a premium. Tarzan knew they must move on to allow the jungle to heal. His family usually migrated in a circular path around the mountain, always returning to this home, and a welcome feast, months later.

But outside pressures had Tarzan on edge. While he feared no living creature himself, he feared what others would do to his family. To avoid areas Tafari's men had tainted and the swathes of jungle the loggers had destroyed, Tarzan would have to lead them to places he had only explored long ago, as a child. And he was not entirely certain what he would now find there.

Thinking about the loggers brought Jane to mind. Tarzan felt comfortable in her company. He enjoyed learning and she had taught him many new things about the world around him. It had been good to have somebody to talk to after many years. The last human contact he'd had was with a French United Nations officer called D'Arnot, whom he had found wounded in the jungle.

The officer had taught Tarzan to speak English and educated him on the dangers from the outside world that threatened his way of life. A firm friendship grew, but D'Arnot was curious to discover where Tarzan came from, so he left one day hoping to find answers and solemnly promised to return. After many months, Tarzan found D'Arnot's corpse, half eaten by the jungle. His friend had tried to honour his promise, but it had cost him his life.

Tarzan hoped a similar fate didn't await Jane. The jungle was a wild and unpredictable place, for anyone.

A coarse bark echoed across the plateau. It was Kerchak, the biggest silverback in the tribe. He walked past Tarzan with an arrogant swagger. The silverback would have been leader of the *mangani* if it weren't for Tarzan, and whenever he went off exploring he left the elderly silverback in charge. But every so often, Kerchak would test Tarzan, checking he was still fit to be leader.

Tarzan maintained steely eye contact with the gorilla. It was a sure sign of aggression. Kerchak roared, baring his huge incisors – each one as long as Tarzan's fingers. The circular scar on Tarzan's shoulder burned as he remembered the fight with Kerchak that had eventually won him dominance, almost at the cost of losing his arm. The great ape ripped up a sod of earth and flung it at Tarzan.

Tarzan didn't react. He just growled in retaliation. Without turning around, he knew Karnath had stopped playing and was cowering at the back of the aircraft hoping there wouldn't be a fight.

Kerchak thought he sensed weakness and took a loping step towards Tarzan. The pair had played such games many times before, but Tarzan was not in the mood today. With the terrible roar of a bull male, he sprang at Kerchak. The gorilla didn't see Tarzan's leg deliver the sweeping kick that knocked his mighty arms aside and suddenly he found himself falling forwards. The next second Tarzan was crouching on Kerchak's back, rubbing the same clod of muddy earth into the gorilla's face.

Tarzan laughed as Kerchak blinked mud from his eyes, then he flipped from the ape's back and landed on top of the aircraft's fuselage, where he beat his chest and roared to the storm clouds. A clap of thunder carried Tarzan's cry across the mountain.

The other gorillas that had been watching the half-hearted challenge hooted as Kerchak loped away to clean himself, casting a venomous glance at Tarzan as he did so.

Tarzan felt no malice towards Kerchak. It was just the old silverback's way of reminding him that they needed to move on and, if Tarzan wasn't going to lead them, he would.

With a sigh, Tarzan watched as Karnath snatched at raindrops falling past the cave entrance. The young ape was one friend he could rely on.

★

'I want to go to Sango,' Jane said to Robbie. She had waited until they were alone in a quiet corner of the bar. The loggers had slowly dispersed after a hard day's graft. Clark and Archie sat at a table, eating and talking together. Robbie and Mister David, the camp's unofficial foreman, had been playing cards until Robbie quit the game after losing too much money to the grinning Congolese man.

'I won't be going for another five days,' Robbie replied. He knew Jane was keen to go to town, but he'd slipped away on supply runs when she wasn't paying attention because he was under strict orders from Archie not to let her leave the camp.

'What's stopping us going tomorrow?'

'I have to work.'

'Messing around with the jeep's engine, that's not

. . .' She bit her lip. She wanted Robbie's help so it was wise not to annoy him. 'I'm sure you won't be missed.'

'Maybe not, but I'm sure your dad would miss you.' Robbie felt sorry for her. He could see she was getting frustrated within the confines of the camp. It would drive him crazy too. 'Look, ask Archie about coming with me next time. We've got the sat phones, maybe he'll be OK if you just ask.'

Jane looked over at her dad. After everything they'd been through together in the jungle it was difficult to be angry with him, but she still resented him limiting her movements. 'Yeah, right!' she scoffed. 'He wants to keep me here like a caged animal!'

Robbie stood up, eager not to start an argument.

'That's because he cares. And after last time . . .' Everybody had been worried when Jane went missing. He wanted to remind her that *he* had also risked his life searching for her. He wanted to point out that she was lucky to have somebody who looked out for her. Instead, he swallowed his irritation. 'Look, if you want to get out of here we could go for a little exploration. Maybe go and find Tarzan.' He was fishing for any lead from Jane that would take them to the crashed aircraft.

'I don't think he wants to be found.'

'Who knows what somebody like him wants?'

Jane opened her mouth to speak, but before she could tell him just how *smart* the feral boy was, Robbie added, 'We should go see him. Check if he's all right. Head up to that plane you say he lives in.'

'So you're saying you're free to wander into the jungle, but not to drive me to town?'

'I'm saying . . .' Robbie trailed off. She was on guard already and any further conversation would just inflame her suspicions. Instead he feigned hurt. 'I was just trying to help, but I guess you don't need it. Goodnight.'

He headed off without looking back.

★

Jane glowered in the corner. Robbie was obviously trying to keep her away from the town, but why was he so keen on exploring the jungle with her? He'd never had any interest in doing so before. She wondered what had triggered this change in attitude but decided that she was going to go to Sango regardless of what anybody else said. She was a free spirit. She smiled to herself – at times like this she wondered just how much of Tarzan's wild behaviour had rubbed off on her.

4.

Robbie had a lot less maintenance to do now that most of the equipment had been replaced. Instead of using his mechanical skills, he had been asked to keep an inventory of equipment going in and out of the camp. He'd much rather be out with Mister David and the crew, felling the valuable hardwoods, but he suspected that Clark was keen to keep him out of harm's way. He reminded himself that it was either this or a study session with Esmée. Robbie preferred this on-the-job training to sitting in the shade learning from her battered books, and at least working the inventory made him a useful member of the team.

He ticked off the items on the supply list. Nothing was missing and nothing was sabotaged. Tarzan had apparently stopped wrecking the equipment like he used to do, in his attempts to scare them off.

The hut door burst open and Esmée leaned in. She

was out of breath and drenched from the downpour that had quickly turned the ground to thick mud.

'You gotta come quick now,' she said, gasping for breath.

'What's wrong?' Robbie asked, suddenly on edge. Esmée didn't answer but darted quickly along the raised wooden walkway that had been constructed a few centimetres over the mud.

'She won't listen,' she finally said.

Robbie rolled his eyes. 'Jane? And you think she ever listens to me? Tell Archie.' As he spoke he heard the growl of an engine as a foot pressed too hard on the accelerator. Robbie felt a sense of dread – surely she wouldn't? He ran past Esmée, around the back of the bar where the jeep was parked.

Or should have been.

The vehicle lurched forward as Jane crunched into second gear.

'Jane! No!' shouted Robbie running after the jeep. He saw Jane glance at him in the mirror and deliberately accelerate. She brought the vehicle round in a wide U-turn. The jeep's rear end fishtailed out in the mud, but Jane spun the wheel and regained control. She grinned at him.

'It's OK. Promise I'll return before it gets dark!'

'Come back here!' Robbie quickened his pace but the jeep was moving at speed now, jouncing over the potholes. The engine screamed as she redlined it. Robbie slipped and fell sprawling into the mud. He was furious with Jane for sneaking off without him and also for the way she was torturing the engine.

'Go into third!' he yelled after her.

With a grating crunch, Jane shifted gear and the vehicle disappeared down the dirt track. Robbie had no idea how he would explain this to Archie.

★

Jane was pleased with herself. She had taken quickly to driving and had to admit that Robbie was a surprisingly good teacher. With him, she'd completed a few circuits around the camp without too many problems but this was the first time she had been behind the wheel on her own. She thought she was doing a pretty good job.

The engine purred now she was in the right gear, and despite the boneshaking trail, but the jeep's suspension could handle it. Even so the sat phone on the seat next to her fell on the floor and she noticed several missed calls on the screen.

Windscreen wipers fought the rain and Jane made sure she slowed a little as the track curved. She had borrowed a map from Archie's cabin when he wasn't there. A blue highlighter pen showed which of the sprawling network of tracks led to Sango. She was pleased with her plan. This was the only jeep in the camp, so they wouldn't be able to follow her and, when she returned, what could her father do to punish her?

She was determined to find out more information about Tarzan's real family. Her research so far had revealed his real name was Greystoke. Since then she had been debating whether she should contact the aristocratic family who still owned substantial swathes of land in England, and held a seat in the House of Lords, to tell them that the rightful heir to the family fortune was still alive. Although it felt like the right thing to do, she wanted Tarzan to decide for himself. She had tried to explain that he had a real family in a far-off land, but he didn't understand. She couldn't explain the concept of money to him either; he simply couldn't grasp why he needed money for a home or food when he had everything he would ever want around him in the jungle free of charge. Maybe he didn't care?

One mystery that nagged at her was why the Greystoke family hadn't tried to find out the truth about their lost cousin. Jane knew the French UN officer D'Arnot had emerged from the jungle and told the world about Tarzan – only to be branded a sensationalist by the world's press. D'Arnot had approached the family to tell them, but they immediately rejected his claims. Is this what D'Arnot had been coming back to tell Tarzan before he was killed in the jungle? Or had he unearthed something more disturbing?

Jane was so caught up in her thoughts that she wasn't paying much attention to the track ahead and the windscreen wipers were not very effective at clearing the glass. Through the blur, she watched as a chunk of the waterlogged embankment on one side of the trail suddenly gave way. A mini landslide of clay rolled down blocking her path.

Jane hit the brakes. The wheels locked and the jeep skidded forwards through the mud, heading directly towards the landslide. She turned the wheel, desperate to avoid a collision, but that just made the vehicle slew sideways.

Something under the jeep gave a loud bang and it jumped in the air. Jane was shunted from her seat, banging her head hard against the roof. Branches whipped the windscreen, then a huge tree limb smashed through the glass, forcing her to throw herself flat against the seat to avoid it.

The engine spluttered then stalled and the jeep came to a sudden lurching halt. All Jane could hear was the rain drumming on the roof. Her heart was pounding, her arms shaking from shock. She rallied her thoughts, annoyed that she hadn't been paying attention to the tricky and dangerous track.

She tried to sit up, but the branch poking through the windscreen was in the way. She crawled along the seat. The door was jammed so she scrambled through the open side window and fell out, head first into mud. She got up and tried unsuccessfully to wipe off the dirt as she assessed the damage.

The jeep had bounced off the trail and careened straight into a tree. The branch that pierced the windscreen was so sturdy that it supported the weight of the jeep, suspending it centimetres from the ground. Jane could see that a shock absorber from the rear wheel was dangling free, but other than that she was surprised there was no other major damage.

'Great. How am I going to get you down?' she said aloud, to no one.

She tried pulling the jeep in the hope that gravity would help dislodge it from the branch, but it was too heavy and her feet just slipped. The vehicle wasn't going to budge.

Jane forced herself to relax and take stock of the situation. She had only been driving for about thirty minutes, so the town was still too far for her to make it on foot without any provisions. She sighed, her plan in tatters. Glancing back the way she'd come, she judged the walk back to the camp wouldn't be too much trouble although her heart sank as she imagined her father's reaction to her crash.

Thinking about her father made her suddenly remember the satellite phone. She looked inside the vehicle and found it on the floor, the screen cracked and useless. She had never had the chance to use it, and that was something else that would annoy her father. She threw it into the jeep, resigned to the fact that she would have to trudge back to camp and explain her actions.

Despite the warm air, the rain still made her cold and a shiver shot down her spine. She pulled her safari jacket around her for warmth, but it offered no protection for her head. Her hair was already plastered across her face, her jeans and trainers were soaked through and uncomfortable to walk in, but she couldn't just stand around. Taking a canteen of water, a torch and machete from the back of the jeep – basic supplies they carried on every trip – Jane reluctantly headed back towards the camp.

The ground was waterlogged, causing her to stumble through deep red puddles that had quickly formed in the tracks. Even covering half a kilometre was an effort. The monotonous sound of the rain pattering across the jungle dampened any other noises but some kind of sixth sense convinced her she was being watched. Several times she stopped and turned, scanning the trees for any movement. One hand clutched the machete to her side.

Screeching monkeys echoed through the trees. In the past she would have relaxed and continued walking, but Tarzan had taught her to listen. He had explained that every noise was the jungle's breath, made by all living things around her. It held a steady rhythm that was only broken when something was amiss. The slightest change was an indication of something bad waiting for the unwary. She listened carefully before understanding that the monkey calls were not their usual playful banter – they were serious warnings.

Something was stalking her.

She was pretty sure it wasn't a lion. Sabor and her pride lived in a secluded valley where the jungle met savannah. They seldom came this far for food.

'Tarzan?' she called out hopefully.

The trees trembled in the rain. She could see no sign of the ape-man and dreaded to think what might be lurking in the branches, staring back. Jane decided it might be safer to shelter in the jeep and hurried back up the trail. In her haste she stumbled on a rock, splashing loudly through a puddle. She caught her balance, thankful she hadn't twisted her ankle, but then spotted something on her hand, a slimy black slug that pulsed steadily. Even as she watched it started to grow – a leech. Jane shivered in revulsion and plucked the creature from her skin. The soft tube exploded between her fingers and blood splashed across her hand.

'Disgusting!' she yelped.

The leech's head was still anchored to her hand, pinpricks of blood dribbling from it. Jane dug in her fingernails and removed the head. The leech's razor sharp teeth pricked her skin. She was about to mutter again when she saw that another four leeches were tangled in her laces, their ugly black bodies squirming to reach the flesh beneath. The puddle must have been full of them.

She was trying to flick them off with the tip of the machete when she noticed something was moving under the leg of her jeans. With slow trepidation she hitched up the denim – and swallowed a scream. Her leg was covered in leeches, all gorging on her blood. Even as she watched, a pair had swollen to twice the size of her thumb and fallen back into the puddle. Jane felt faint from nausea.

Suddenly she heard movement behind her. The leeches were instantly forgotten.

Robbie jogged down the track, weighed down by a backpack filled with provisions and camping supplies that would see him through the three-day trek to Sango. He seriously hoped that Jane would honour her promise to return by nightfall as he had no desire to sleep rough just to catch her up, but he needed to be prepared.

Clark jogged beside him. The older man was already panting and beneath his wet rain poncho his shirt was dark with sweat stains. He insisted that they slow down. He was carrying the same heavy pack as Robbie, with the added weight of a rifle slung over his shoulder.

'Won't that girl ever learn?' he growled between breaths.

Archie had been furious when he'd heard what Jane had done, but his anger had quickly subsided after she'd failed to answer her sat phone. Alarmed, he blamed himself for forcing her into acting so rashly.

'Why did I bring her here?' he kept repeating to himself.

Robbie had grown up without a father figure, at least not a decent one, and he hated seeing Archie like this. It just reminded him of Jane's lack of awareness about how she affected the people around her.

'We'll go an' fetch her,' Clark had volunteered.

Robbie had been surprised to find himself included in Clark's offer. He was quite happy to wait for her to return, since she was more than capable of looking after herself – she was a quick learner and stubborn with it, he thought. But Archie wasn't convinced Jane could manage driving the off-road route. The deciding factor had been that Sango was simply too dangerous a place for her to be walking around on her own. She might as well throw herself to the savages of the jungle.

They pressed on in silence, heads bowed, through the relentless rain. Trees either side of the track arced above them, forming a tunnel. Ahead, branches hung across the track, freshly snapped in half by the passing jeep.

Robbie was paranoid that Jane had been going to the Internet café in Sango to dig up more information about him online. When she had told him that his stepfather had survived his impulsive attack, he had briefly felt elated. To learn he was not a murderer lightened the weight of guilt that had been smothering him since he fled home. The euphoria lasted for several days before reality sank in that he would still be wanted for attempted murder – then the dark moods that descended upon him were worse than ever.

Attempted. That was the word that burned in his mind. The man who had slowly killed his sister with his callous brutality, the man who hadn't peeled himself off the sofa while Sophie was dying in the next room, was still alive. Not only alive – he had now turned Robbie into the bad guy.

How is that fair? he ranted to himself. His brief time in the jungle had shown him the harsh balance of nature. Only the strongest and smartest survived – yet in the so-called civilised world, awful people like his stepfather still lived in peace.

'Look out!'

Robbie was so wrapped up in his thoughts he only just had time to leap out of the way as a flash of yellow and a blood-curdling roar bolted from the trees and slammed into his companion.

It happened so fast; Clark was still reaching for the rifle slung over his shoulder when the leopard crashed into his backpack. Its talons ripped the bag open, spilling the contents. As the fabric tore, the leopard slipped and razor-sharp claws slashed across Clark's thigh, drawing blood. He screamed in pain and collapsed, which caused the leopard to lose its balance and roll away, splashing through a puddle.

Robbie stood frozen to the spot. He hadn't expected the attack. Gathering his wits, his hand went for the machete hanging from his belt.

Clark was already pale through loss of blood. He tried to slide the rifle off, but the strap was caught in the tatters of his backpack.

Powerful muscles rippled under the cat's golden fur as it clambered back up on all fours and, driven by the scent of blood pumping from Clark's leg, it rounded on its prey.

Robbie raised the machete as the leopard coiled to spring. No matter how sharp it was, the long blade didn't offer much of a defence against the beast's teeth and claws.

Then a chilling bellow echoed across the jungle – the sound of a savage battle cry. The leopard reacted instantly, its ears falling flat in terror as it tried to pinpoint the source of the noise.

Hope surged through Robbie as he recognised the call. His gaze still fixed on the leopard when he caught a movement in the trees. Out of the darkness,

Tarzan dropped on to a nearby branch and yelled his challenge once more.

It was a perfect distraction. The leopard didn't see the dark shape bolt from the jungle behind it. A black panther sank its claws into the leopard and both animals splashed through the mud, locked in a ferocious tussle.

'Sheeta?' Robbie said incredulously, recognising the sleek black panther as Tarzan's feline companion, who often fought by his side.

The clamour from the duelling animals was deafening as they rolled on the ground. Sheeta was not only more powerful – he was also a superior hunter. He dug his teeth into the back of the leopard's neck. The bite was not intended to kill, but served as a sign of dominance that the other cat understood. With a yelp, it sprang from Sheeta's jaws and fled into the jungle. The panther roared triumphantly; there was no need to follow.

Tarzan leaped from the tree. It was a six-metre drop, but he landed gracefully and ran his hand over Sheeta's head, scratching him between the ears while mumbling soothing words.

Robbie realised he was still frozen to the spot with the machete. He pulled himself together. 'Thanks,' he said earnestly, but Tarzan didn't appear to be listening. Robbie stabbed his blade into the ground and ran over to Clark. The wound in Clark's thigh was so deep, Robbie felt sick just looking at the blood soaking through his trousers.

'I'm going to need to bind it,' Robbie said. He knew the importance of treating wounds out in the jungle. Just the smallest infection could kill a healthy man. His hands were covered in mud, so he washed them in the rain as best he could. It was far from hygienic, but it would have to do. He fumbled for the waterproof first-aid kit that had fallen from Clark's pack. 'Tarzan, I need some help here.'

Tarzan made no effort to intervene as Robbie pulled a packet of cotton gauze from the kit, tearing open the sterile packaging with his teeth. He pressed them against the wound.

'Tarzan! Please!' He knew Tarzan had no love for the loggers. He only tolerated them because of Jane. Robbie half turned and saw Tarzan disappearing into the foliage. 'Come back!' he yelled as he pressed Clark's wound together. He couldn't believe Tarzan would leave someone to die. 'Tarzan!'

'Forget 'im,' said Clark through gritted teeth. 'Survival of the fittest is all he understands, right? We're all just meat in 'is eyes.'

Robbie tried to press the wound together, ignoring the wet sound the blood-soaked flesh made under his hands. Clark gasped in pain.

'Press here while I find a bandage.' Robbie was becoming frantic and worried his fumbling would make the wound worse.

Tarzan emerged from the trees with several broad leaves. He roughly nudged Robbie aside – which felt like being shoved by a boulder – peeled back the blood-soaked pads and covered the wound in a thick sap he squeezed from crushed leaves.

Clark sighed in relief. 'It's made my leg numb,' he said.

Tarzan wrapped the leaves around Clark's thigh and bound them with thin vines, pulling them so tight that Clark yelped.

'I felt that!' Clark breathed heavily, but he was alert. With shaking hands he examined the improvised dressing. 'Thanks, mate,' he croaked.

'Clark live. Go back,' said Tarzan pointing towards their camp.

'We can't,' said Robbie.

'Too dangerous here,' said Tarzan gravely. 'Tarzan does not watch Robbie all day.'

'We can't go back, because Jane stole our jeep to go to town.' Robbie pointed down the trail, hoping that Tarzan understood at least some of the words.

He did. His eyes narrowed as he repeated one. 'Jane?'

Then he bounded into the trees without another word.

★

Black fumes poured from the outboard motor as a rusting speedboat bounced across the choppy waters of the Congo river. Nikolas Rokoff sat at the prow, enjoying the wind brushing his face. Paulvitch sat in the middle, his head hung over the side as he felt another bout of seasickness churn his stomach. They had been travelling on the river for the best part of two days and were relieved when they turned yet another meandering bend to find the town finally coming into view.

The boat's captain skilfully brought them level with a crowded jetty surrounded by dozens of other vessels, all of which had seen better days. The strong river current forced him to keep the throttle high until Rokoff had secured their mooring. The Russian shoved a fistful of Congolese francs into the captain's grubby fingers and pointed to the five large silver flight cases in the boat.

'Put them ashore and guard them with your life. If anything goes missing, I'll have your hand off.' Although his tone was calm and measured, the captain had no doubt Rokoff would stick to his word. His eyes flicked to the black-handled serrated hunting blade that hung from Rokoff's belt. He judged that it was more than capable of slicing through bone.

Paulvitch staggered on to the jetty. His trembling legs forced him to reach for a wooden post for support. Rokoff didn't give him a second glance. He was studying the town. Once a ramshackle fishing village, its location on the bank of the river had made it a well-placed hub for people travelling through the jungle. The village grew into a town as a thriving black market overtook fishing as its largest business. Rokoff liked it. It had the atmosphere a Wild West frontier town would have possessed, he imagined. It was the end of the road for civilisation, surrounded by expansive jungle in which Okeke's prize lay.

But that was not the reason he was here. Any good hunter could do the task Okeke had set. Rokoff was here to hunt a prize that had eluded him in the past.

He would have the head of the legendary white ape, no matter what the cost.

Jane was rooted to the spot as the trees shook all around her and harsh grunts came from the foliage. A familiar sense of fear returned as dark shapes flitted in the treetops. The rain dribbled into her eyes and made it difficult to see, but she could clearly hear the grunts turn into shrill calls that conveyed aggression from her unseen opponents. She raised her machete, although she did not know how effective it would be.

The trees shivered once more and a chorus of high-pitched screeches drowned out any other sounds. Their intensity increased, the prelude to an attack that Jane expected at any moment.

But it didn't come.

The foliage behind her split apart and something huge burst through, sailing over her head and landing in the mud on all fours. It took a second for her to recognise Tarzan. The ape-man now stood between Jane and her unseen enemy.

Tarzan's stomach heaved as he bellowed, punching his fist repeatedly into the mud. It was a fighting display she had seen the silverback gorilla Terkoz perform once when he clashed with Tarzan. This time, it appeared to have the desired effect on whatever was lurking in the bush. With a sharp screech, the trees shook defiantly one last time, then Jane's stalkers retreated with a loud crack of branches. The jungle was silent once more.

'Tarzan!'

Only when Tarzan was satisfied the enemy had gone did he turn to look at Jane. His brow was furrowed with anger.

'Jane nearly died alone here! *Targarni* are bad. Dangerous!'

Jane was startled by his harsh words. 'I had this.' She held out the machete. 'And I wasn't originally planning on taking a walk out here. I crashed the jeep.' She wanted to ask what the *targarni* were, but Tarzan interrupted.

'Robbie come for you now.' He studied her carefully. Jane self-consciously followed his gaze to the leeches on her leg. In the last few terrifying moments she had forgotten about them. Now they were fat with her blood and fell harmlessly into the mud. While she was still repulsed by them, Tarzan's news was worse.

'You saw him? He's going to be mad when he sees the jeep.'

Tarzan must have seen her worried expression, because he started to smile.

'Jane in trouble?' There was a mischievous twinkle in his eye.

Jane didn't want to dwell on Robbie – she had had dozens of questions for Tarzan since she last saw him. Why hadn't he come back to the camp? Should they tell his real family that he was alive? She had her own ideas and theories but, now he was standing before her, she didn't know how to begin. Instead she found herself asking about Tarzan's adopted family.

'How's Karnath?' She had been there when the lion had killed Karnath's mother and often thought about the little ape.

'Karnath miss Jane. You want to see?'

Jane's heart leaped. She had longed for an opportunity to return to the paradise high up in the cloud rainforest. A silent nod was all it took for Tarzan to lift her on to his back and into the trees. She gripped tightly around his neck as they hurtled through the jungle. Rain stung Jane's eyes as Tarzan gained speed, leaping upwards from tree to tree to gain height, then running to the slender ends of branches that he used as springboards to sail across yawning gaps in the canopy.

Jane had been terrified when she first travelled this way in the dizzying heights of the jungle. Now she found it exhilarating. She still had to force herself not to flinch when branches whipped close to her face, but she trusted Tarzan. He had been doing this all his life.

They made a quick stop off at the jeep for Jane to leave a message for Robbie, then Tarzan took them deeper into the jungle.

She wasn't sure how long they had been travelling. It could have been an hour, possibly two. Tarzan didn't slow his pace for a minute. They climbed higher up the side of a tree-clad mountain, passing through the heart of the storm that was drifting from the peak into the valley below. As soon as they broke through the low clouds, a vivid blue sky greeted them and Jane felt the tropical sun on her face.

Tarzan leaped from a branch and snagged a liana to slide on to the plateau he called home. He gently put Jane down and she couldn't help but smile. It was exactly as she remembered. Most of the gorillas had climbed to the lake shore below to forage, but the few who remained near the aircraft recognised Jane and gave low welcoming grunts of reassurance. A steady drum of footsteps across the earth made her spin round – just in time to see Karnath leap at her.

Jane caught the little gorilla in her arms and almost fell backwards.

'Wow! Karnath! You've grown.' The young ape threw his arms around her, hooting excitedly. Jane laughed. She couldn't remember anybody ever greeting her so enthusiastically. Tarzan certainly hadn't. Karnath played with her blonde hair and she had to pull some out of his mouth. 'Don't eat my hair!'

Tarzan smiled, taking simple pleasure in seeing his friends reunited. Cradling Karnath in her arms, Jane walked out on to the plane wing that hung over the edge of the plateau like a diving board. The dizzying height no longer bothered her and she found the view across the caldera as breathtaking as ever. Now the rain had passed, the air was thick with birds and insects. Gorillas moved around the foot of the waterfall below, seeking food. Jane focused her attention on listening to the environment: Karnath's excited breathing; the faint thunder of the torrent; the occasional hoots from the gorillas; the menagerie of birds calling from the rich jungle. It was like something out of a dream.

'I love this place,' she said.

She was suddenly aware of Tarzan standing close behind her. Even though she was listening she hadn't heard his footsteps.

'*Mangani* must leave this home,' said Tarzan sadly.

'Why?'

'Need food. Stay too long here.'

'Where will you go?'

Tarzan pointed to a range of mountains. 'Tarzan travels to new lands. You will come?'

Jane hesitated. Trapped at the camp, she had longed to go on another adventure with Tarzan, but now she wasn't so sure. Her head was bursting with questions that needed answering. If she asked Tarzan to return her to the camp, then she wouldn't have time to get any more answers from him. The note she'd left in the jeep's engine explained that she may be gone with Tarzan for a day or two – she hoped that was long enough to find out more information from him.

'What's at the mountains?' she asked.

Tarzan shrugged. 'Tarzan only go when young. Dangerous place.'

'So why there? There must be lots of places for them to eat.'

Tarzan pointed from the direction they had travelled, back to the camp. 'Because father of Jane destroy best lands.' He looked straight at her with his piercing grey eyes; they suddenly had the steely look of a killer. Even though she trusted Tarzan with her life, Jane was still frightened by his sudden shifts in mood.

'You want him to stop? You want him to go?' she asked.

Tarzan nodded, then hesitated as he thought about the words he was using, a difficult task since he had not spoken in weeks. 'He only live because he your father.'

The statement sent a shiver down her spine. There was no emotion in his voice, just cold reason.

'If he left, I would have to go with him. We wouldn't see each other again.'

Tarzan hesitated, his brow knitting with a flash of sorrow. Again, he picked his words with care.

'Tarzan not want you to go.'

'I don't want to go either.' A month ago she would have been shocked to hear herself utter those words, but now she spoke them with conviction. 'But . . . if I had to . . . maybe you could come with me?'

Tarzan shook his head dismissively. 'Tarzan home is here.'

Jane hadn't wanted to speak so soon about what was on her mind, but she seized the opportunity.

'You have another home with your real family – the Greystokes in England.'

She had expected him to get angry, but instead Tarzan looked bemused and gestured to the apes. 'This Tarzan's family.'

Jane opened her mouth – then shut it again. She

47

had tried to explain that there were people out there who would be desperate to know he was alive, but he refused to understand.

'I think D'Arnot spoke to your family, your human family, and told them you were alive.' Tarzan's face darkened at the mention of his friend. Jane pressed on. 'I think he returned to the jungle to persuade you to go back with him. To prove to them that you were alive.'

For a long moment Tarzan said nothing. An awkward tension hung in the air and Jane feared that she had overstepped the boundaries of his patience. Karnath sensed the atmosphere and jumped from Jane's arms so he could roll around Tarzan's feet, reeling head over heels. The little gorilla's clowning brought a sharp laugh from Tarzan. He ruffled Karnath's head.

'Tarzan belong here.' He looked long and hard at Jane, then his expression softened. 'This Tarzan's family. I care for them, not Greystoke.'

★

Clark's injury slowed them considerably and it took the best part of two hours to reach the crashed jeep. Robbie was dismayed by the damage Jane had inflicted on the vehicle and it took another hour to fix the damaged shock absorber. Robbie kept a small toolkit in the back of the vehicle, but it wasn't the best equipment for such a task. However, with a little ingenuity and a lot of brute force, he managed to reattach it. It took a further forty minutes for him to get the jeep off the tree branch by hacking at the thick wood with his machete, eventually managing to cut just enough for the weight of the jeep to snap it.

Clark had been forced to watch from his seat on a rock. Whatever herbal remedy Tarzan had given him to ease the pain had worked to a degree, but now the slash on his thigh was throbbing under the improvised bandages.

While examining the engine, Robbie found a folded piece of paper wedged under cables. He recognised Jane's handwriting and admired her thinking. Under the bonnet was the driest place in the car and the one place Robbie was sure to look. He sighed loudly as he read it.

'What's she gone and done now?' asked Clark.

Robbie read out the note. 'Gone with Tarzan, don't wait up. Two days max.' He screwed up the paper and threw it into the footwell. 'She's just asking for trouble.' He also held up her sat phone. 'Smashed.'

Clark shook his head. 'She's as stubborn as her mother. At least we know she's safe. Don't think there's a safer place in this whole damn continent than with him.'

Robbie bristled. He'd always treated Jane as a surrogate sister and tried to look after her as such. Clark's comment made him think that he'd failed. He felt a pang of jealousy towards Tarzan. The ape-man was making him feel worthless.

'Could be a good thing too,' said Clark thoughtfully, then he suddenly hissed with pain and clutched his leg. Whatever Tarzan had given him to numb the soreness was rapidly wearing off. 'I'd better get this looked at. It's startin' to sting. Few leaves and monkey spit are OK, but I'd prefer professional medical attention an' I'm only gonna get that in town, ain't I?' He was referring to the *Médecins Sans Frontières* base in Sango. That the international medical aid organisation had established a post in Sango showed what a remote and desperate place it was; otherwise it would have no access to medical care. 'Least we can drive there now.'

Robbie helped Clark into the passenger seat. 'So why is Jane wandering off into the jungle a good thing?'

'Because Archie won't like it. It's all very well gorilla-boy savin' us now an' again, but it's not the kinda company he wants around Jane. This is good ammunition, mate. Maybe we can start bringin' him

around to our thinkin'. If we could mobilise everyone at the camp we could be a step closer to findin'
that plane. Find that and we got proof we can show
'em. In the meantime, I wanna make a few more en-
quiries about this *soutpiel*.' Robbie didn't understand
the derogatory South African term, but he could
guess what Clark meant.

There was little conversation during the drive to
the town as both were lost in their own thoughts.
Clark was imagining the reward they could claim for
delivering a British lord, while Robbie wrestled with
the idea of using Tarzan as a tool to get rich. If Tarzan wanted to hide away in the jungle then so be it.
It was exactly what Robbie was doing, so he understood the desire to be left alone. And Tarzan had now
saved them on more than one occasion, so he felt in-
debted to the wild man. However, a nagging jealous
voice pointed out how much better it would be not
to have Tarzan around to upstage him and how much
his life would improve with the reward money. Perhaps he could even head to Australia to start all over
again.

It was late into the afternoon when they arrived
in Sango. The transition from the isolation of the
jungle to the bustling, polluted town always jarred
on Robbie. The single-storey buildings were nothing
more than wooden huts with corrugated-iron roofs.

Power and phone cables hung low, zigzagging across the potholed dirt roads that were piled with rubbish. A few stray dogs picked amongst the litter and looked up hopefully as Robbie climbed out of the jeep. The aromas of civilisation hit him hard: cooked food, petrol generators and open sewers. It was over-whelming.

He left Clark at the doctor's office – just an open gazebo with grubby canvas sheets draped around it for privacy. There was a queue of people waiting on benches in the shade. Robbie quickly glanced ath them and saw eye infections, terrible sores and a host of grim-looking injuries made all the worse by the tropical climate.

Robbie headed for the café containing the town's only Internet connection and waited patiently for the man using it to finish.

'*Izvinite*,' said the man as he nudged past Robbie in his haste to leave.

Robbie didn't recognise the language, but wasn't surprised. People came to this lawless town from every culture around the globe. He intended to use the thirty minutes' Internet access he'd paid for to do a little more digging on the Greystokes. He angled the screen so that the café's young owner couldn't see what he was looking at.

Several pages came up about the story he now

knew well. Just over a decade and a half ago, Lord and Lady Greystoke had been flying over the Congo when their plane was lost from radar and never found. He glanced through reports of the French UN officer, Paul D'Arnot, who claimed to have discovered the mythical white ape that haunted the jungle and who was in fact the son of the Greystokes. Without evidence, the Frenchman was scorned by the media and placed under psychiatric evaluation before he disappeared, never to be seen again.

It was the same research he had printed out for Clark and, after fifteen minutes, he concluded they had everything the Internet had to offer on Tarzan and the Greystokes. He was about to leave when he suddenly had a thought. Jane had used the Web to discover that Robbie's stepfather was still alive and that the police were searching for him. It had never occurred to him to check for news about himself. Robbie typed in his own name and hit 'search'.

Ten minutes later he quickly left the café and headed to the jeep. His mind was racing with conflicting thoughts of anger and fear over the new information he had just discovered. He didn't know what to do, or who to turn to.

Should he tell Clark? After all, Clark had deliberately not wanted to know anything about Robbie's past. He didn't even ask any further questions when

Jane had let slip about his stepfather. How would he react? He was afraid that Clark's opinion of him would sour and he would risk losing a friend and mentor. The only person he could speak to was Jane, but did she already know about the things he'd just read? If so, why hadn't she told him? Was she trying to protect him? Then again, every time she tried to raise the issue, he changed the subject. That made him feel rotten. Here he was, using Jane to extract information about Tarzan, and all the while she was looking out for him. He knew he was being an awful friend and he was now certain that he was in terrible trouble. Far worse than he'd ever suspected.

On his way out of the café he failed to notice that the man who had bumped into him earlier was sitting at a table inside drinking a beer. He had been positioned at just the right angle to observe what was on Robbie's screen. Once he was sure the boy had left, Nikolas Rokoff stood up and crossed over to the computer. With a few mouse clicks he called up the web browser's history and rapidly read through all the pages Robbie had visited . . .

7

Jane looked out in awe. Never had she seen a land-scape that looked so beautiful or so deadly.

They had been on the go for several hours, mostly in Tarzan's preferred high-speed mode of travel through the canopy. Sometimes Jane clung on to him as he performed death-defying leaps, other times she felt confident enough to run along broad branches and make the smaller jumps to trees whose boughs intersected. She was unable to match Tarzan's ener-getic parkour-style ballet through the dizzying heights and he often had to stop and wait for her to catch up, but he was always patient, never com-plaining. Jane caught glimpses of their destination as they travelled, but she was not prepared for its full beauty, revealed only when they emerged from the dense foliage on to the very edge of a cliff top.

A volcano poked up from the lush landscape, plumes of fine grey smoke drifting from it. The conical peak was black and barren and, as Jane watched, glowing coals of rock spat out and rolled down the scree. A thick tangle of vegetation clung midway down the volcano's flanks. There, in the fertile soil, it was denser than ever.

They were now deeper into the heart of the jungle than Jane had ventured before. Flocks of African grey and red-fronted parrots circled the cliff, filling the air with noisy chatter.

'Thunder Mountain,' said Tarzan.

'And this is where you want to bring your family?' Tarzan nodded. The volcano was clearly active, and although the rich rainforest around indicated that it hadn't erupted for a long time, she was concerned about Karnath and the others living under its shadow. 'Are you sure it's safe here?'

Tarzan peered down into the jungle below. His brow creased with concern. '*Targarni* here, but food for us all.' As he spoke he plucked a green fruit from the tree and tossed it to Jane. She hadn't realised how hungry she was until she bit into it. Tarzan crouched next to her, surveying the land. He seemed lost in thought as parrots landed close by and watched them with intelligent eyes.

'D'Arnot like this place,' he suddenly said.

Jane was astonished that Tarzan had willingly

offered this vague piece of information. She encouraged him. 'Tell me about him.'

Tarzan hesitated, as though he was both wrestling with the idea and groping to find the words. Jane didn't hurry him and, after a lengthy pause, Tarzan began his tale. It was difficult to follow with his limited vocabulary, but Jane slowly learned the story of how D'Arnot and Tarzan had met.

*

Years ago, a younger and smaller Tarzan dropped from a tree and lay bleeding on the jungle floor for a considerable time. He felt weak and dizzy from the substantial loss of blood from a terrible shoulder wound courtesy of Kerchak's powerful bite.

The beast had fought with Tarzan's ape mother, Kala, in a petty display of dominance. It was a pointless tantrum, and it had led to the accidental death of Kala's newborn daughter. Even though he suspected he was no physical match to the silverback, Tarzan had flown into an uncontrolled rage.

With his vine rope and a knife that he'd found on the body of a dead tribesman, Tarzan attacked Kerchak with every ounce of strength he possessed. He sank the blade into the silverback's folds of fat several times, yet that did little more than irritate him. Tarzan was agile, but all it took was one chance blow from the gorilla's mighty fist to crack the boy's rib. While he was down, Kerchak bit deep into his shoulder. The ape was aiming for his neck, but Tarzan had managed to move aside enough to save his life. His only chance of survival was to flee.

Pulling himself upright, Tarzan tended to his injuries, clipping the flap of shoulder flesh in place with the snapped-off heads of angry army ants. While bathing the wound in a stream he heard gunfire. He was familiar with the noise, which accompanied humans prowling through the jungle slaughtering animals – not for food, but for pleasure.

Tarzan was in no fit state to confront the intruders, but his curiosity got the better of him. He carefully pushed through the foliage towards the sound. There he found a man, alone, and judging by the sound of his ragged breathing, he was injured. As Tarzan crept silently closer, he pictured the situation ahead just by listening to different sounds. The man was afraid, mumbling under his breath. Cold steel clicked and clacked as he fumbled to reload a rifle. But what was he afraid of?

Only when he was metres away did Tarzan pick out the subtle movement of branches and a familiar low growl. His old foe, Sabor, was hunting in the highlands again.

Tarzan had defeated the young lioness once before

in a terrible tussle by using his vine rope to choke her as he slashed her flanks with his knife. If she chose to fight again today, when he was already injured, then he would undoubtedly die. Tarzan was not afraid of death, that was the way of the world, but he had no desire for it so soon. There was still too much for him to explore and discover. Death could wait.

Tarzan positioned himself at a good vantage point to watch as the lioness circled the man, who was slumped across a log. The rifle in his hands was shaking so badly that the ammunition was scattered on the floor. He groped for the cartridges, but his fingers seemed unable to grip properly. Tarzan could now see why. Sabor had taken a bite from his left upper arm. The man's sleeve was soaked in blood and its smell was enticing the beast to attack again.

The lioness crouched ready to spring. Her hindquarters twitched in anticipation. The man's death was imminent.

Tarzan roared as loud as he could, beating his chest with his good hand. He bounded from the tree and landed between the man and the animal. In his weak condition, Tarzan almost passed out from the effort. Concentrating hard, he unsheathed his knife so Sabor could get a good look at it and snapped the vine rope like a whip.

The lioness roared with fury at being denied an

easy meal. Tarzan didn't flinch as the animal's warm, meaty breath washed over him. Instead he stood tall and swept the blade through the air. Sabor was stubborn, but not stupid. With a snarl she retreated into the foliage as fast as she could.

Tarzan's head was swimming as he turned to face the man. Ordinarily he would not bother to save any of the hunters he encountered in the jungle, but there was something about this man that was different. His clothing was a patchwork of greens that made him blend into his surroundings; the only splash of colour was his bright blue beret. The man's mouth hung open in a look of utter astonishment, an expression that Tarzan would never forget. It made him laugh every time he recalled it. That was how he always remembered D'Arnot.

D'Arnot would never forget the boy who appeared from the jungle and frightened off a hungry lion, then turned to look at him and laughed as if nothing had happened.

In the following weeks, Tarzan nursed himself and D'Arnot back to full health. The man was older and took longer to recover but, when he was able to walk properly, Tarzan took him back to his ape family.

Kerchak greeted them both with a hostile territorial display. It was the first time the silverback had seen Tarzan since their fight. Tarzan gave no sign of fear but kept low and stared at the ground, motioning for D'Arnot to do the same. It was a sign of sub-ordination so Kerchak begrudgingly left them alone and D'Arnot could roam freely across the plateau. His astonishment at being amongst wild mountain gorillas, and effectively welcomed into their band, was overshadowed when he saw the aircraft con-cealed by the jungle. He had hundreds of questions – none of which Tarzan could answer, so in the months that followed, D'Arnot patiently taught Tarzan how to speak. Based on what he found in the aircraft, he'd concluded the boy was from England, so they learned English, but he would have preferred to teach him his native, more elegant French.

Tarzan picked up English quickly and even taught D'Arnot some Swahili words he had learned from shadowing hunting parties and loggers through the jungle. The Frenchman was fascinated to discover that Tarzan had developed his own language and often pointed out animals on their frequent treks for food: *gimla*, the crocodile; *manu*, the monkey; *lano*, for the annoying mosquitoes.

After a couple of months, they were able to have lengthy and coherent conversations. The Frenchman marvelled at Tarzan's intellect and was often on the receiving end of the boy's short temper when he failed to find the correct word to communicate.

D'Arnot followed the band of gorillas as they migrated around the huge mountain in search of pastures new, eventually coming back to the plateau after many months. In that time, the Frenchman made no attempt to leave the jungle. He often asked Tarzan what he remembered of his past, particularly his family, but as far as the boy was concerned, the ape Kala was his mother. Tarzan was more interested in learning about D'Arnot.

'Why you here?' he would ask.

'I was part of a United Nations peacekeeping force in this country. We call it the Democratic Republic of Congo. We came here to monitor the peace efforts after the second Congo war and then we were assigned to watch over the Ituri conflict.' The names were unusual to Tarzan, but over the last few months he had gauged some idea of what the world was like beyond the jungle. 'I was on patrol with my unit when we were attacked by *Lendu* soldiers who had fled into the jungle. I was the only survivor. When Sabor attacked . . . I was a dead man. I owe you my life.'

Tarzan didn't understand the gravitas of that statement. He was content with calling D'Arnot a friend.

Since the jungle had no seasons, measuring the passage of time was almost impossible. D'Arnot could tell he'd been there a while because Tarzan had grown almost as big as him and his language skills had greatly improved. The Frenchman had shared his combat and survival skills with the boy and been surprised to learn new techniques from Tarzan. With their combined knowledge they often hunted food together, although the Frenchman was no match for Tarzan's stealth or speed – and didn't share his love for raw meat, so he ate only plants and vegetables.

On one such hunting trip at the river's edge, D'Arnot revealed something that had been growing in his mind. 'I must leave.'

Tarzan longed to explore the vast savannahs of Africa and visit the cities with trees made from stone.

'Go where?' asked Tarzan.

'Home.'

'D'Arnot is home.' It was a simple, innocent declaration that made the man's heart break.

'My home is in France – Lyon, a beautiful city with wonderful Roman ruins. You should come.'

'How many days' travel?'

'Many . . . But listen, Tarzan, understand that if you come with me then there is a chance you may not ever return here. You may not want to.'

Tarzan was confused. 'Why?'

D'Arnot gestured to the aircraft. 'You must have been on board this when it crashed. Even if your real parents died on it, there will still be people who are concerned about you. They probably think you're dead.' D'Arnot had found references relating to the Greystokes around the plane and had told Tarzan about their charitable work. 'The Greystokes are a powerful family, known around the world. If you are one of them—'

'I am Tarzan. This is my home.'

D'Arnot could think of nothing to persuade Tarzan to come with him, but had no intention of lying to the boy. As much as D'Arnot enjoyed the jungle, he didn't belong here, and Tarzan knew that. It was time to return to civilisation and reclaim his old life, as well as recount the amazing story of the boy who lived with apes. It was with a heavy heart that D'Arnot parted from Tarzan.

They walked to the edge of the *mangani* territory at Thunder Mountain. D'Arnot assured Tarzan that he could find his way through the jungle safely from there, now that he was armed with the knowledge and skills the boy had taught him. Tarzan did not wish to leave his jungle family, nor did he want to see D'Arnot leave. The officer solemnly promised to return once he had made contact with the outside world and they said their goodbyes. Tarzan watched his friend climb down the cliff-top track. D'Arnot turned and waved before disappearing into the jungle below.

Tarzan waited until the sky turned dark, watching for any sign of D'Arnot's return. He sat alone, his heart burning with feelings of abandonment he didn't understand. That was the last time he saw his friend alive.

★

Tarzan's head hung with sadness as he finished recounting the story of his past to Jane. It had been some effort to recall words he learned once but had not used in a long time, while reliving the emotions of D'Arnot's departure.

Jane laid a hand on Tarzan's shoulder in a gesture of comfort. She knew he feared that she would disappear like D'Arnot. She wanted to reassure him, but the truth was she did not know what would happen in the future and she did not want to lie to him.

For a long while they sat in silence. Parrots circled overhead, and Jane found herself lost in the relaxing jungle sounds. The wind changed direction and Jane started to smell sulphurous fumes from the volcano, though it was faint enough not to be unpleasant. However, it seemed to set Tarzan on edge and he climbed onto a spire of rock projecting from the cliff, his eyes scanning the jungle below.

The sky was bleeding red as the sun slowly sank behind the mountain ridges and Jane fought to stop yawning. She had almost forgotten that her day had started by stealing the jeep from the camp.

'Maybe we should be heading back? It's getting dark.'

'Jane stay.'

'Will she?' she said, half smiling.

'Yes.'

Jane opened her mouth to speak, but stopped. She thought it unlikely that they would have been able to make it to the camp tonight and had anticipated, hoped even, that they would sleep on the plateau and head back to the camp the following morning.

Tarzan said nothing more as darkness cloaked the land and the sky was filled with stars – clusters of diamond dust across the infinite blackness. It was so dark Tarzan was just a shadow next to her. Under any other circumstances, Jane would be terrified, sitting out in the middle of the jungle at night, but with Tarzan she felt safe.

Tarzan suddenly spoke. 'See!'

Jane thought he was referring to the stars and was about to reply – then realised he was pointing at the volcano. A dull red glow shone from the crater and she saw cracks appear across the top of the cone, and the occasional fountain of lava. Every so often red cinders flicked in the air like a swarm of fireflies then a chunk of rock would be ejected over the rim in a ball of cherry-red flame and roll down the side of the cone, breaking apart in a colourful display.

'It's beautiful!' Jane exclaimed. She had never seen anything like it before, but she was thankful they were viewing it from afar.

They watched for some time as the waxing moon rose, illuminating the landscape and allowing Jane to see Tarzan properly. She was alarmed to notice he was staring into the jungle.

'What is it?' she whispered.

For a moment, Tarzan didn't speak, then he whispered back, 'We are hunted.'

A chill ran down Jane's spine. 'By what?'

'*Targarni*.'

Tarzan's head cocked left then right as he tracked a noise beyond Jane's hearing. She became conscious of just how loud her breathing sounded. She took a deep breath and held it.

The night chorus of jungle insects was deafening. Frogs chirped with melodic calls and the faint bass rumble of the volcano underlined nature's score. Then she heard it – a definite movement in the trees. But it wasn't just one hunter.

The trees suddenly exploded with a hideous high-pitched screech she had heard earlier as she walked along the trail to the camp. Dozens of pale faces loomed in the moonlight. Tarzan issued a roar so primal and raw that Jane was astounded any human could make such a noise.

Before they had a chance to move, the ambush was sprung.

The speed of their attack was incredible. Jane saw
fleeting glimpses of the dark shadows and terrible
pale faces but she instantly recognised them as chimpanzees. These were not the clown-like animals she
had seen on television back at home. They were
wild, savage killers. Even on all fours they came up
to her chest. Black fur rippled over powerful muscles
and their lips pulled back to reveal lethal teeth that
could easily tear her apart. Worse, they were clearly
hunting as a pack. The ambush was an intelligently
planned operation.

Tarzan blocked the first attacker as it barrelled towards Jane. She heard the meaty thud of two bodies
impacting at high speed and saw the chimp rebound
into the darkness.

Another pair wheeled around Tarzan, shrieking
wildly. He caught one by the throat as it leaped for
him, its teeth chomping fiercely. Tarzan used the

chimp as a shield against the second. Other members of the band kept back, hooting in the darkness to add to the chaos.

The chimp Tarzan was using as a shield sank its teeth into his arm. With a grunt of pain, Tarzan hurled the chimp at the second attacker and was rewarded with cries of pain from them both. He lunged after them, roaring fiercely.

Three more chimps suddenly bolted out from the trees, heads bowed low. They charged at Tarzan with such force that his legs were swept from under him and the mighty jungle warrior was flipped through the air. The moment Tarzan crashed to the ground, the three chimps set upon him with a ferocious volley of blows.

'Get off him!' Jane screamed.

She was no match for the powerful apes, but she couldn't watch Tarzan suffer like this. She took a step forward, her mind searching for possibilities, and her foot struck a boulder, hidden in the dead foliage. Jane lifted it with difficulty, as it was almost the size of her head.

Sharp teeth bit into Tarzan's arm and he roared with pain and fury. Jane could see blood on his face and only hoped it wasn't his own. With shaking arms she raised the rock under her chin, ready to throw.

Then something made her turn – and the sight

chilled her blood. Moonlight reflected from the ghostly image of a huge chimpanzee. It was a head taller than the others and clad in pure white fur. One eye was swollen almost shut, but the other burned red with murderous intent. The albino chimpanzee was obviously the troop leader and stalked along the edge of the cliff in a calculating manner. It now occurred to Jane that she was the intended target and the other apes had attacked Tarzan as a diversion.

Jane's instinct was to scream – but to her amazement her voice exploded as a terrible bellow as she threw the rock.

The albino hadn't been expecting resistance, but he leaped aside just in time and the rock bounced before pitching over the cliff.

Jane's cry sent Tarzan into a frenzy. He stood up, bearing the weight of the three adult chimpanzees that still held him. He punched one in the side of the head, forcing it to release the vice-like bite it had on his other arm. Then he headbutted the ape clinging to his chest and struck it unconscious. The last creature was holding on to his back with a long arm around his neck, its teeth reaching for his scalp. Blood was dripping into Tarzan's eyes but that didn't stop him from bounding forward and shoving Jane to the ground as the albino sprang.

Tarzan and the albino clashed in mid-air. Tarzan

twisted his body so that the chimp clasping his back met the full force of the impact. It was enough for the animal to shriek and let go. It made a hasty retreat, limping into the trees.

But the albino was not so easily deterred – it recovered faster than Tarzan and, with a loud screech, swung straight at him.

Jane could only watch as the two figures rolled on the ground at the cliff edge. The gang of chimps around her screamed and whooped to encourage their leader, but made no effort to join in.

Tarzan and the albino traded a flurry of blows. Tarzan was pitched on his back and the albino seized the opportunity to pin him down.

But that was exactly Tarzan's plan. As the albino made his move, Tarzan planted his feet firmly in the chimp's stomach and kicked. Jane could hear ribs breaking as the squealing albino was hurled against a huge tree with such force that the trunk shook. Tarzan had intended to hurl him off the cliff top, but nevertheless, victory was his.

The albino staggered into the darkness. Moonlight reflected from its ghostly face as it snarled in defiance before disappearing into the jungle. The other chimpanzees followed with low murmurs, defeated, tearing through the undergrowth like a band of hoodlums.

Tarzan thumped his chest and roared victoriously.

Jane ran to his side, alarmed to see the network of cuts that now decorated his body. His face was painted in his own blood, but despite this he was grinning at his success and showed no signs of pain. Jane knew words of comfort were meaningless. Instead, she indicated after the chimps.

'*Targarni*?'

Tarzan nodded and looked out towards the volcano. 'This *targarni* land.'

Jane felt terrible. To feed his family, Tarzan was being forced to lead them into dangerous territory. Forced because her father refused to leave the jungle he was systematically destroying, pushing the apes away from familiar grounds.

Jane couldn't stop the anger welling up inside her, nor could she shake off the guilt that she had persuaded her father to stay just so she could see Tarzan again.

★

'I'm not happy about this,' said Archie. 'She's been gone for over a day! She could be hurt. She could be . . .'

'She's with Tarzan,' stated Clark. 'You know what that means. She's in the safest place on the continent.' He rubbed his bandaged leg as he spoke and gazed out of Archie's cabin window at the morning sun rising above the treetops. He was on powerful pain-killers, but even those did little to dull the throb that surged up his leg. The doctor in Sango had praised the improvised medical attention Tarzan had given the wound after the leopard attack. Clark had been careful not to mention the wild man, referring to him only as a local. The doctor was smart enough not to ask any questions. In the middle of the Congo the less you pried the safer you were.

Archie was deeply worried.

'Clark's right,' chipped in Robbie. 'And she said she'll be back soon.' He had no intention of looking for her, because he knew she would fare better with Tarzan than he would alone. Besides, he could hardly concentrate on the conversation about Jane because his own thoughts and imagination were reeling from what he had discovered in Sango. Now, he was desperate to head back to New York and confront his stepfather again, but thinking rationally he realised it would be a terrible mistake. Not that he could even afford to make the journey. Not yet. But the reward money they expected to get for revealing Tarzan's existence . . . that would solve everything. Money would give him the options to make the right decision.

He also needed to speak to Jane, now more than ever. She was the one person who knew his whole secret. The only person he truly trusted. When he drifted back into the conversation, Clark was speaking. After delivering the news that Jane was with Tarzan, he'd had to calm Archie down by letting him in on the plan to claim the reward money.

'Told ya before, mate. There's nothin' much ya can do to stop her so don't bother. Focus all your energies on this venture. We need it to work, so don't go thinkin' about jackin' it all in again.' Archie looked guiltily away. That's exactly what he had been thinking. Clark tapped the desk for emphasis. 'We spent too much on this last round of equipment. There's no bailin' now.'

'Do you realise what you're saying?' said Archie quietly. 'This is my daughter we're talking about.'

Clark glanced at Robbie. Robbie looked away. He could tell, from the way Clark leaned forward and dropped his voice conspiratorially, that he was outlining his plan again.

'As I see it you have three choices for your *bakvissie*,' Robbie knew bits of South African slang, with which Clark often peppered his conversations, but not this. Evidently he was referring to Jane. 'One, you leave her be and hope she's safe out there. Two, try and stop her but you'll have better luck tryin' to stop an *olifant*. Third, we do the right thing and help Tarzan – which is exactly what we're doin'. He's got a family waitin' for him.'

'I know, I know,' said Archie with a sigh. Robbie felt a twinge of guilt. Clark had been really playing the family card to bring Archie on side and it was working. Clark's intentions seemed honourable, but they were driven by greed.

'We have the same problem though,' said Archie wearily. 'We don't know where Tarzan is and, as you've said, without evidence who'd believe us? If you recall, we didn't believe Jane when she told us.'

'Things have changed. We can find the aircraft ourselves,' said Clark with a smile.

Archie frowned. 'How? None of us have that skill. We could spend a lifetime out there in the jungle and never come across it.'

'Fortune is smilin' on us, mate. We found some folks who need our help. And they've come 'ere.' Clark grinned at Robbie. Robbie couldn't meet Archie's suspicious gaze. Their logging operation was illegal and secret. The idea of bringing somebody into Karibu Mji went against all their own rules which is why Clark had no choice but to mention the plan to Archie.

'You've brought people here?' said Archie in surprise.

Clark gave a dismissive wave of the hand. 'Relax.

They're conservationists, heard 'em in Sango askin' about gorillas and we got to talkin' about a trek. They're with Esmée. Come on, let's chat with 'em.'

Archie scowled at his old friend. Bringing anybody new to the camp risked exposing them, so Archie was furious his friend had made the decision without him.

They left Archie's office and headed across the camp to the bar. Clark struggled with a wooden crutch that Mister David had improvised for him when he returned, but it was still difficult to cross the mud and elevated walkways with just one good leg.

Robbie walked slowly behind. Movement on the edge of the tree line caught his attention and he was surprised to see Jane walk out from the trees as calmly as if she had been out for a morning stroll.

'Jane!' Robbie couldn't help shouting her name.

Archie looked round and saw his daughter. He immediately ran to gather her up in a huge hug. Then he held her at arm's length and looked her up and down. There were flecks of blood on her clothes.

'Are you OK?' His voice was heavy with concern.

'I'm fine!' Jane smiled and indicated the blood. 'Don't worry, it's not mine.'

'What happened?'

'Tarzan found me at the jeep.'

'The one you stole?' Clark pointed out. He didn't

want Archie to forget that Jane had brought this all on herself.

Jane looked suitably guilty. 'Yeah. Sorry about that. I just needed to go to town. This place was starting to feel like a prison.'

Archie hesitated. He knew from experience that if he complained it would only make her more defiant.

She looked sheepishly away. 'I left a message. I knew Robbie would find it.'

She flashed him a smile, but Robbie didn't feel in the mood to return it. He felt bitter; he'd always been on hand to help Jane, but the moment he needed someone to confide in she wasn't around.

'I was with Tarzan. You knew I'd be safe.'

Archie swallowed his sharp reply. Jane noticed Clark's bandaged leg.

'What happened?'

'Bit of a story behind it. I had to go lookin' for some selfish girl who stole my jeep. This is the thanks I get,' he patted the leg, 'when a leopard tried to take a chunk outta me.'

Jane looked down at the ground and mumbled, 'I'm sorry.'

'Bit late now,' said Clark harshly. It was the only way he knew of making Jane open her eyes to see the trouble she'd caused. 'Luckily, our friend Tarzan was around to help out. I would very much like to find him and give him my thanks.'

Clark looked into the trees in case Tarzan was hiding and watching, but Robbie suspected he would have quickly departed once Jane had arrived safely back at the camp. Clark turned to Jane pointedly.

She stared back in defiance. 'I'll let him know.'

Robbie could see that Jane was suspicious of Clark's clumsy attempts to get her to lead him to Tarzan. Now, more than ever, Robbie needed Jane to be on his side, and setting aside his feeling of anger, he gave her a hug and forced a smile.

'It's good to have you back and in one piece.'

Jane smiled. 'You wouldn't believe where we went! There's an active volcano out there.' She gestured vaguely to the jungle. Robbie saw Clark's eyes widen as he mentally stored that titbit of geographical information in case it helped their search for Tarzan. 'And there's a real white ape! It's an albino chimpanzee. Maybe the legend doesn't refer to Tarzan after all?'

'You saw it?' Clark asked curiously.

Jane pointed out the blood on her clothes. 'It attacked us. Tarzan saw it off.'

Archie looked uncomfortable. The thought of his daughter placing herself in danger terrified him. Before he could deliver any moral lessons, which Jane would probably misinterpret as him interfering, Robbie butted in.

'Let's go and get something warm to eat. I bet you could do with it.'

A few electric lights and several broad glass-less windows illuminated the bar, but it was still dingy inside. Esmée was preparing a stew for the loggers. She looked up when Jane entered and a smile lit up her face.

'Look at you! Welcome back, girl. You had us worried.'

'I know. I didn't mean to, but . . .' Jane trailed off when she saw the two strangers at a table near the bar.

Robbie helped Clark to their table then offered a chair to Jane before he sat down. He couldn't help but think the men were studying Jane as if she were an animal.

'This is Nikolas Rokoff, and this is Alexis Paulvitch,' said Clark, introducing each man in turn. Clark jerked a thumb at Archie. 'And this is the boss-man, Archie.'

Rokoff stood up and firmly shook Archie's hand. 'A pleasure, sir.' Then he turned to Jane and lightly took her hand, giving a gallant bow. 'This must be your daughter? Charmed to meet you. I have heard quite a lot.'

Paulvitch didn't stand, but nodded in greeting.

Robbie could see the confusion on Jane's face. The camp's strict rule of secrecy had been drummed into her.

'They're searching for mountain gorillas,' explained Robbie. He felt Jane tense next to him.

Rokoff smiled pleasantly. 'We're conservationists from Lomonosov Moscow State University. We're working with colleagues from Kampala in Uganda, researching mountain gorilla population numbers. You see, there are fewer than eight hundred left in the world, so the rumours of unknown groups out in the wild are significant.'

Jane didn't say a word. Esmée placed a plate of stew in front of her but she didn't touch it even though her stomach rumbled, triggered by the rich smell.

'I was told you had spent time out in the jungle and seen them.'

Jane stiffened and glanced at Robbie as he spoke up.

'That's right. That's where she was last night, right, Jane?'

'You were out, with wild gorillas?' said Rokoff.

He peered at Jane as if he was trying to guess her secrets.

'She has a friend who looks after them,' added Robbie.

Jane glared at him. Rokoff leaned back in his seat and stroked his beard thoughtfully.

'He's also a conservationist,' exclaimed Jane.

'Indeed . . .' replied Rokoff, almost in a whisper, with a far-off look in his eyes. Then he looked back at Jane and smiled. 'A fine fellow, I am sure. We would be honoured to exchange research notes with him.'

'That's not going to happen,' said Jane flatly.

'Nevertheless, I would like the opportunity to hear for myself whether or not he refuses to cooperate. I am particularly interested to know if he has seen or heard of the legendary white ape.' He said the last two words slowly and they sounded thick with his accent. His eyes scanned across her bloodstained clothes.

'Now there's a coincidence,' said Clark. Robbie's eyes stayed fixed on Jane. He could see her glower, willing Clark to shut up. 'Jane was just talkin' about her run-in with it. Ain't that right?'

Rokoff looked at her with a half-smile. 'So the legends are true?'

'I . . . I don't know what he means.' Jane stood up. 'I'm feeling pretty tired. I'm going to get some sleep.'

She walked out, head bowed. Only Robbie saw her angry expression and he felt the bonds of trust between them dissolve. Robbie's cheeks flushed as a deep sense of guilt washed over him.

'Remarkable,' said Rokoff.

'Sorry about that,' said Clark. 'She's got a stubborn streak she inherited from her mother. Right, Arch? Esmée, some Tuskers here.'

Rokoff took the offered beer and clinked the neck of the bottle against Archie's. 'To independent children. You have brought up a fine woman. I believe this is your camp?'

Archie took a long swig of beer as he sized Rokoff up. 'You're aware of what we do here?'

'I'm not blind,' said Rokoff.

'No. And you're not mute either. Why would a conservationist turn a blind eye to all of this?'

'As I explained to your companion,' Rokoff gestured to Clark, 'my interests are very *specific*. In a country such as this, you cannot afford to make enemies of those you need to work alongside. You and your people are at the forefront of exploring this wilderness and see things I can only wish I could. You're not poachers, and while I don't agree with logging, I assure you that my interest lies purely in the gorillas and not you. Not this.' He waved his hand around the room. 'Your daughter has given me confirmation enough that we are exploring the right area.'

'Could you track down the gorillas without her?' asked Clark as innocently as he could.

Rokoff laughed. 'There is not a creature on this planet I could not track. You only have to know where to start.'

Clark emptied his bottle and slammed it on the table, beaming.

'Excellent. Then I reckon you're welcome to hang around here, eh?' The question was aimed at Archie who had been studying the two men with suspicion.

'I suppose so,' Archie finally conceded. 'But we value our privacy. If you endanger that, then you won't be so welcome.'

Rokoff nodded amiably. 'I understand.'

Clark clapped his hands together. 'Great. If you want the gorillas then it'll help us find what we're looking for.'

'Which is?'

'An old crashed aircraft.'

Rokoff smiled and extended his hand. 'It sounds like a fine partnership.'

Robbie remained silent as the two men shook hands. Archie still didn't look as convinced as his old friend Clark. Robbie was now beginning to feel the same way.

Despite the humidity, Robbie shivered. It was as if they had just struck a deal with the devil himself.

Robbie felt increasingly uneasy with the new pace of events. He hadn't believed for a moment that Jane really needed to sleep, but he left her alone until midday to cool off. Esmée unsuccessfully tried to gather them both for a lesson, but since Tarzan had made his appearance she was finding it harder to pin down either Robbie or Jane.

Jane sat at the edge of the camp gazing at her phone. In the past, she would have been writing emails to friends back home. Now she used the phone to type in information she had gathered about the Greystokes. She had started to spend hours pondering over it.

She was so absorbed in her research that she only noticed Robbie when his shadow fell over her. Still angry, she deliberately ignored him.

'How long are you going to keep this up?' She

remained silent. Robbie sighed and sat next to her. 'You can't be mad at me for ever.'

'I wouldn't be so sure about that.'

Despite the atmosphere, Robbie couldn't help but smile. That was more like the old Jane.

'We're both stuck out here whether we like it or not. There's not a whole lot of space to get mad in.'

Jane put her phone down and stared at him. Her jaw muscles tensed as her anger built. 'I can't believe you told that . . . that stranger all about Tarzan!'

Robbie held up his hands defensively. 'Wait a second. I never mentioned Tarzan. He was looking for the gorillas.'

'They are Tarzan's family!'

'And Rokoff's trying to help them.'

'They don't need help!'

'I don't see what you're so crazy about. Surely it's a good thing that people are trying to help the gorillas? Tarzan won't be around for ever . . .' Jane looked up sharply. 'You were the one who suggested telling the Greystokes about him. What if he decides to leave?'

Jane looked away, but Robbie caught the hint of regret.

'He's better off here. Better off without us interfering,' she said quietly.

Robbie was thankful that she didn't see his face in case his reaction roused her suspicions. She didn't know that he and Clark had already contacted the Greystoke estate and had received an answer demanding proof of their claims.

'Shouldn't he make his own mind up about that?' Robbie asked gently.

Jane looked at him suspiciously. 'What do you care?'

'He's saved my life, quite a few times now. I owe it to him.' Robbie spoke the truth, but not the whole truth. What was left unsaid made him feel sick with guilt. However, Tarzan was not his only problem right now.

'Jane. I need your advice.'

Jane abruptly stood up. 'My advice is to leave him, and me, alone.' She stormed off across the camp.

'Jane!' he called after her, but she ignored him.

Robbie was angry. The whole Tarzan situation was detracting from what was really important. He'd do everything he could to help the Russian find the stupid gorillas and the aircraft – then he'd have the proof they needed to claim a reward for bringing Lord Greystoke home.

Then Robbie would be able to set about getting his life back on track.

★

Before Jane returned to the camp, Tarzan had made

an arrangement with her so she could contact him. He showed her an animal trail that cut across the camp and was relatively easy to follow. After an hour on foot, it opened into a wide clearing with ancient trees circling a dust bowl at the foot of a smooth, gently curving cliff face. The trees were hollow, long dead and devoured by insects. Tarzan called it a Dum-Dum. He beat out a specific rhythm on one of the trunks with his fists and the sound reverberated through the hollow tree; a deep bass which bounced from the curved cliff to amplify the sound across the jungle.

Jane was entranced; it sounded like melodic thunder. Her first attempts were pretty ineffective and left Tarzan laughing so hard that tears streamed down his face. She tried using a stick but it broke on impact, sending Tarzan into more fits of laughter. She found a sturdier branch and eventually got the hang of beating out the rhythm he showed her. If she wanted to contact Tarzan, she just had to beat the tattoo on the Dum-Dum and he would hear.

Jane felt claustrophobic in the camp. Robbie's attitude had annoyed her and she didn't like the look of the two Russians now hanging around. They had brought their own four-by-four, a huge modern Land Cruiser with tinted windows. Two days passed and they hadn't asked Jane any further questions, partly because she avoided them whenever she could. They never appeared to be doing much and just stayed in the camp, killing time. A couple of times, Rokoff had marched into the jungle, but he was never gone for very long. Their blatant inactivity raised Jane's suspicions.

She couldn't visit Tarzan; she knew he was busy persuading his family to move to fresh feeding pastures. However, with Rokoff lurking around, Jane wanted to warn Tarzan more with each passing day. She hoped he was at least within range of the Dum-Dums, so after several days she decided to slip away.

Rather than upset her father any further, she told him about her plan.

'I might be away for a day or two,' she said when she'd finally got him away from Rokoff and Clark. She had expected the usual bluster, but he just nodded and looked a little sad. 'I'll be with Tarzan, so . . .'

'So you'll be OK.'

She had anticipated more of an argument, and his resigned attitude surprised her. She gently squeezed his hand. 'Thanks, Dad.'

Jane took a machete, a rolled-up rain poncho, a full water canteen and a few provisions in a backpack, then headed to the Dum-Dum.

The sun beat down and made the jungle blossom

around her. Colourful birds and insects swooped through the trees and monkeys chattered in the distance. Despite the swarms of insects, it was a pleasant walk and she found it difficult to remember why she had hated the forest when they first arrived. She beat her tattoo on the Dum-Dum and sat back to wait.

After an hour she sensed she was being watched, although she couldn't identify exactly what was bothering her. Her eyes scanned the jungle and the feeling intensified. It felt almost hostile.

Then Tarzan leaped into the clearing, landing neatly on all fours at her side. He didn't utter a single word, but his eyes narrowed as he scanned the trees too.

'What's out there?'

His face looked grave. Time seemed to stretch as they listened in silence. Then Tarzan slowly stood and pointed further along the animal trail.

'Bad men come this way,' he said. 'Come.'

He headed along the track, barely making a sound. They didn't travel far before Tarzan raised his arm in a signal to stop. Jane couldn't see what the danger was until Tarzan broke a branch from an overhanging tree and tossed it ahead.

The tripwire was practically invisible, but the moment the branch broke the wire's tension, the trap was sprung. With a terrible slashing sound, a rope noose contracted and plucked the branch from the ground, lifting it high in the air. It was simple and brutal.

'Who would do something like this?' exclaimed Jane.

'Poachers.' The word growled at the back of Tarzan's throat. He indicated down another trail. Through the bushes Jane could see a deer had triggered another trap and was swaying in mid-air, its neck broken.

They all hunted meat to survive, but this was cruel. While the camp meat came from the jungle, Archie insisted that they should never use snares and killed only as much as they needed for food. She had seen Tarzan hunt with his bare hands, but he too only took what he needed. Poachers hunted in excess and often for the animals' pelts rather than for their meat.

'What would poachers be doing so far in here?' asked Jane. She was worried that poachers this close to the camp could mean trouble.

'Your father. He bring these men here!'

'No, that's not true. Nobody at the camp would do this.'

Tarzan was unconvinced. 'Then why poachers here? Never come this far!'

Jane knew he was right. Something had pushed the poachers deeper into uncharted terrain. They weren't the first strangers to turn up and the coincidence was a little too much.

'Two men arrived at the camp. Rokoff and Paulvitch,' she said. 'They're Russians who claim to be conserv— They study animals. They want to know where the gorillas are.'

Tarzan was instantly wary. 'Jane say no?'

She hesitated and Tarzan's face fell.

'I didn't say anything!' Jane said hastily. 'Robbie mentioned there were some out here. He was only trying to help,' she added quickly. She surprised herself at how easily she was defending him. 'They wanted to know how many gorillas are alive.'

'They do this?' He pointed at the deer trap.

'No.' She wasn't entirely convinced by that but had no desire to condemn the Russians to the wrath of Tarzan when she had no proof. 'They've spent time out in the jungle, but this . . . ?'

Tarzan shook his head in silent disagreement. He understood much more about jungle life than he was able to articulate. They carefully approached the dead deer and Tarzan cut it down with his knife. He reverently laid the animal on the ground. Its body was cold, a kill from the previous day. Anger blazed in his eyes and Jane felt anxious. She had seen Tarzan ruthlessly kill his opponents in jungle battles, and she feared that the death of an innocent deer could propel him into a rage.

'Tarzan . . .' she reached out a hand and laid it on his arm, hoping to soothe his temper. She had barely spoken when Tarzan quickly turned, raising his head attentively.

'Poacher here!' he whispered.

Jane's blood froze. Encountering poachers had not been on the day's itinerary.

'We should hide!' She quickly bolted back down the trail, in the opposite direction from where Tarzan was looking. She thought it was the same path they had taken through the foliage and only realised her mistake at the last moment when Tarzan yelled out.

'NO!'

With a terrible crack, Jane heard a trap trigger around her. A rope whipped passed her ear, drawing blood from her cheek. Suddenly she felt a rope bind her knees painfully together and hoist her into the air. Pain coursed through her legs as she dangled upside down from the tree. A scream escaped her involuntarily. Even with her ears ringing she could still hear the sudden clamour in the bush and raised voices as the poachers zeroed in on their target.

★

Nikolas Rokoff adjusted the sight on his sniper's

scope and brushed a bead of perspiration from his forehead. The dense jungle forced him to follow his quarry closely, which meant he had to take extra precautions. Leaves and branches obscured most of his view, but he could see enough of Jane hanging from the trap.

Stupid girl, he thought. He had taken an instant dislike to her the moment they met. *A typical self-absorbed teenager*, he thought.

Then he saw eight poachers emerge from the bush and gather around her. They were all locals, armed with machetes and guns. Their eyes lit up with delight when they saw the new prey they had caught. They jeered amongst themselves and poked her with gun barrels until she was slowly rotating. With a flash of silver, a machete was teased along her throat as the men enjoyed frightening her.

Then Rokoff felt a shudder of excitement as a wild bellow resounded through the jungle. He had never heard such a creature before. Its call conveyed unquestionable dominance over the land and even the expert hunter felt his blood run cold.

Through the scope he saw rapid movement. The poachers turned on the unseen enemy, and gunfire cracked across the jungle. One was wrenched backwards into the undergrowth and Rokoff could hear his screams abruptly extinguished.

The remaining poachers wheeled around to where their companion had vanished and automatic gunfire chewed the undergrowth apart. Rokoff watched in amazement as another poacher was hoisted into a tree by a rope that quickly tightened around his neck.

Even the girl, still dangling in mid-air, was helping to add to the confusion. She snatched a rifle from the poacher closest to her and hit him in the face with the butt of his gun. The man collapsed. Another hunter tore the rifle from her hand. Rokoff was forced to modify his opinion of her; she had a feisty spirit.

With his attention on Jane, Rokoff missed another two men get swallowed into the jungle. He marvelled at the shrewdness of their assailant. The three re-maining men gathered fearfully around Jane. One plucked the rope from her hand and another, evid-ently their leader, shoved his rifle barrel into her ribs and shouted in Congolese French.

'*Rends-toi ou on la tue!*'

Nothing seemed to happen and the men twitched nervously, jumping at every sound the jungle made. Tension grew as the men glanced around, wondering where the next attack would come from.

Rokoff blinked. A knife suddenly embedded itself in the lead poacher's forehead. He twitched and fell to the ground. The men looked at their fallen leader in horror. It was just the break their attacker was looking for.

A muscular figure charged through the under-growth on all fours and cannoned into the poachers. For a moment, Rokoff thought he was looking at a bald gorilla but then he adjusted the scope and focused on the deeply tanned, toned body, which was covered in a lattice of scars – some old, some quite fresh. It was certainly human.

The wild man's hands found the poachers' throats and drove both men to the floor. Rokoff was no stranger to violence and regretted that his view hid the details of how the savage dealt with his victims. Judging from the expression on Jane's face, it was brutal.

Rokoff smiled and turned to Paulvitch, who hunkered down beside him. He too had been observing the battle, grinning as if watching a movie fight rather than a real encounter with real lives at stake.

'The legends appear to be true, at last,' breathed Rokoff. He shook his head in wonder then turned to Paulvitch. 'This puts Okeke's prize in the shade.'

Paulvitch looked worried. 'He's paying good money. Better in my pocket than in his.'

'Don't worry, my friend. We'll fulfill his contract. My prize won't be caught so easily, but now at least the game can begin.' He looked back down the sniper's scope and watched as Jane was freed from the trap. Rokoff couldn't take his eyes off the wild man. He had never seen anything like him before. 'I may have just found the perfect adversary.'

10

'Robbie, where are the Russians?'

Robbie looked up and was surprised to see Jane. Archie had told the camp not to expect to see her around today. It was raining and he had sheltered under a wooden porch on the edge of the camp, rather than in the bar with the rest of the loggers. Now Jane was standing in front of him he was suddenly aware that it looked as if he was waiting up for her. With a horrible twinge of realisation, he thought maybe that was true.

'They're around,' he answered, trying to keep cool.

'They're not in the bar,' said Jane.

'Do I look like their chaperone?' said Robbie irritably. 'Maybe they're in their cabin?'

Jane looked over at the cabin Archie had offered the Russians. There were no lights on. Robbie followed her gaze and thought back to when he had last seen the men.

'To be honest I haven't seen then since . . . since I last saw you.' He pointed to the edge of the camp. 'Their car is still here so they must be around.' He noticed that some of the equipment was missing from the roof. He stood up and walked to the end of the porch. Jane followed him. She had spotted the missing gear too. 'They must have gone somewhere.'

'There were poachers not too far from here.'

'Out here? Did you see them?' Jane didn't meet his gaze, a sign that told him something bad had happened. Then he noticed the fresh cut close to her ear. 'Are you OK?'

'I got caught in one of their traps. I think they were going to kill me.'

'But Tarzan . . . ?' He didn't even need to finish his sentence. Jane just nodded. 'Then they're not a problem any more, are they?'

'I told Tarzan that Rokoff had come here and was asking about gorillas. With the sudden arrival of these poachers . . . he's suspicious. And I don't blame him.' She stared at the Land Cruiser thoughtfully. 'We should look inside. It might give us a clue to their whereabouts.'

They walked over to the vehicle. The rain was now a gentle drizzle, but it seeped easily through their clothes, making them shiver. The vehicle was locked.

'Well, it was a good idea,' said Robbie. 'Now let's go and get dry.'

'Can you force it open?'

Robbie gave her a measured look. 'Back in New York, I was a mechanic, not a car thief. Don't get the two mixed up.'

But Jane didn't need Robbie's help. She picked up a rock and went to hurl it through the driver's window. Robbie clamped his hand around her wrist.

'What're you doing?'

'I want to look inside!'

'You can't just smash your way in. This doesn't belong to you.'

'Then what do you suggest?'

Robbie sighed. Jane was forcing him to do something he didn't want to do – yet again.

'Give me a second.'

He ran to the camp's bulldozer. He had been servicing the engine earlier in the day and had put a metal toolbox underneath to keep it out of the rain. He returned with a pair of long-nosed pliers and a length of strong wire. He inserted the pliers at the top of the door and used his weight to open them, wrestling the two handles in both hands. There was a crack of stressed metal – then the top of the door frame inched open. Robbie fashioned the end of the wire into a hook and slid it through the gap. The wire was just long enough to reach the door lock. It took several attempts, but he finally snagged the door lock-release bolt with the hook and pulled. The door opened.

'See? Better than brute force.' He carefully bent the top of the door back into shape. The paint was cracked, but it would fool a casual observer.

They climbed inside the vehicle, thankful to be out of the rain. There were more equipment boxes in the back, matt-black impact cases, which usually held delicate instruments.

'So what do you expect to find?' said Robbie. 'Some dead animals?'

Jane opened the nearest small case. It was empty. The packing foam inside was sculpted to hold something about the size of her satellite phone. Another, larger box was similarly empty. Jane climbed over the seats so she could get amongst the long narrow boxes. Robbie stayed in the front keeping watch. Now they were both in the car, he realised he had a captive audience.

'Jane, I really need to speak to you.'

'About what?'

'About my stepdad.' Robbie was thankful that Jane suddenly stopped and looked at him with concern. 'He's looking for me.'

Jane gave him a little smile. 'That's hardly surprising. You did try to kill him.'

Robbie hung his head – he wasn't proud of his actions.

'But look around you. He's not going to find you here. The world's big. Lots of places to hide.' She continued opening cases, assuming her consolatory words were effective.

'I've done a little digging around,' said Robbie as she opened another case.

'Really?' Jane was only half listening. 'Looks like they've taken everything.'

'The police know I fled the country. They know I stowed away on board a cargo ship in New Jersey.'

Jane looked at him in surprise. 'How?'

'They tracked my movements on CCTV. It took them a while. But they know I'm in Africa.'

Shocked, Jane now turned her full attention on Robbie. 'Are you sure?'

'They've posted a "wanted" picture. But it gets worse. My stepfather has been giving news interviews about me. I saw one on YouTube . . .'

He trailed away. Jane encouraged him to continue, then noticed that he was looking at the box in her hands.

Inside was a large hand-held device, about the size of their phones. Robbie realised that another similar device must have been in the first empty box. The letters GPS were emblazoned on it. But that wasn't all. Jane must have accidentally brushed the 'on' switch when she had opened the case. A blip flashed in the centre of the screen.

'Let me see that,' said Robbie taking it from her hands.

'It's just a GPS.' Jane had seen many since her father had set up the camp. 'Nothing special about that.'

'This is a very expensive piece of kit. Military grade.' Robbie had searched through equipment catalogues with Archie when they moved camps and had seen the price of high-end equipment. It was way beyond their budget. 'Which means it's extremely accurate.'

Jane shrugged. She didn't know why he was getting so excited. She tapped the blip on the screen. Latitude and longitude numbers were highlighted above it. 'What's this?'

'Our current location.'

Robbie opened the car door and stepped out, ignoring the rain, which had gathered pace again, and stared at the screen. He reached the bulldozer and looked back at the jeep. The blip had moved. As he slowly turned around he lined up the GPS with the Land Cruiser. Then he ran back to the vehicle.

'Give me your jacket,' he demanded.

Jane looked at him as if he was demented. 'What?'

'Take your jacket off!'

Jane reluctantly did so. She was only wearing a T-shirt underneath, but the rain had soaked through to her skin anyway. Robbie began searching her pockets.

'What are you doing?'

'Didn't you ever watch any films?'

'No. I have friends and a life,' Jane answered, sarcastically. 'Or had,' she corrected herself.

The pockets were empty. Robbie was just starting to think he was being paranoid – then his fingers found something under the collar. He unfolded it revealing a small metal disk pinned there. He took it off and showed Jane.

'What is it?' she asked, confused.

'A GPS transmitter. The kind of tag you use to track animals. Watch.' He gestured towards the screen and threw the disk away from the vehicle. The blip on screen moved as the disk landed in the mud. 'Rokoff is tracking you.'

'But why would . . . ?' She knew why. Luckily she had only been to the Dum-Dum and back.

In the moment's silence, the rain turned once more into a downpour and beat against the metal roof. Robbie's stomach churned as he thought about his part in the betrayal. He didn't believe for a second that a pair of conservationists would stoop so low. Jane turned to the longer cases. She flipped the nearest one open. It was empty, but the sculpted foam inlay clearly revealed the definition of a rifle.

'No!' gasped Jane. Then, without warning, she bolted from the vehicle and ran across the camp.

Robbie raced after her. He slipped several times in the mud but caught his balance. Jane found her footing with ease and gained distance.

'Jane! Stop!'

She wasn't listening. Impenetrable dark jungle loomed at the edge of the camp and Robbie quickened his pace. Jane finally tripped on a stump in the darkness and fell into the mud. Robbie reached her side and helped her up, clutching her arm as tightly as possible to stop her from fleeing.

'There's nothing we can do right now!' Robbie shouted over the driving rain. Jane tried to pull away from him. He could see the anxiety across her wet face and was unsure if she was crying. She struggled a little more.

'The Dum-Dum!' she shouted. Robbie looked at her blankly. Jane shoved him in the chest, pushing him backward. 'Get a torch! We have to try!'

Robbie wanted to argue. Running into the jungle at night was a reckless thing to do – but the expression on Jane's face reflected the guilt he was feeling for bringing Rokoff to the camp. He knew it was his fault — but he had no idea just how bad things were about to get.

★

In the mountains, the deluge of rain sounded like a herd of animals migrating through the jungle. Tarzan watched as little Karnath sat at the entrance of the aircraft fuselage, peering out and snatching at the heavy raindrops, trying to eat them. Tarzan chuckled and settled back on the folded branches that formed the nest he had created for the night. Unlike the gorillas, Tarzan preferred to sleep on the ground whenever he could, and favoured the seclusion of his artificial cave even more. A few of the gorillas shared the cave and it was turning into a peaceful night as the regular patter of the rain lulled them all to sleep.

Tarzan's eyes suddenly flicked open. His keen hearing picked up something no ordinary man's could. He crept to the cave entrance and crouched beside Karnath. He strained to listen — then heard it again. It was a faint grunt from Kerchak. Something was bothering the old silverback.

Tarzan ruffled the soft, greasy fur on Karnath's head then walked outside. The rain masked Kerchak's grumbling, but Tarzan tracked the old silverback to a large rock where he sat under the bows of a great tree to shelter from the storm. The silverback cast a glance at him and snorted, then gazed back into the darkness. Despite their clashes, they held a begrudging respect for one another.

Tarzan climbed next to Kerchak and listened for what was bothering the old ape. This close, Tarzan could smell wild garlic on the silverback's raspy breath as they peered into the darkness. The wind blew the rain against them, dampening any telltale scent or sound of what was agitating them.

★

Through the night-vision goggles, the vivid red and orange thermal signatures of the apes stood out in sharp relief from the cool blue-green background of the jungle.

Nikolas Rokoff lay downwind. His body was so tense that the only movement was the beating of his heart. He had been watching the gorillas since he'd crawled through the mud into position an hour ago.

He was delighted his plan had worked so flawlessly. His original intention of hanging around Sango to grill the locals for information on the mountain gorillas hadn't been necessary as luck had led him straight to the Canler boy browsing the Internet, looking up details about the Greystokes. Once Canler had left the computer, without taking the precaution to delete his browsing history, it had been a simple task for Rokoff to review the web pages. Gathering intelligence was critical to a successful mission and he suspected there might be something helpful in the boy's research.

He carefully read through the information relating to the Greystokes, and absorbed the stories about a murderer on the loose in America. Why was Canler so interested in this? He made a mental note of that in case it should prove useful at a later date. Then he found the relevant pages, about the legendary white ape said to haunt the jungles of the Congo.

This was the very reason Rokoff was here. Once he had chased such rumours and left empty-handed. The story still plagued him as if the wild foe was taunting him, determined to be the one creature he would never be able to hunt. Finding Canler in Sango had been a stroke of luck and his hunter's sense told him he was on the right track. From that point, it had been simple enough to talk loudly about the apes and ensure his path crossed with Clark and Robbie at the nearest bar so he could ingratiate himself with them.

While pulling together the logistics for his mission, Rokoff had arranged rapid transportation from the jungle, which was always difficult in a backwards country. He paid the local poachers to comb the area for any signs of the gorillas. Their instructions were simple: if they encountered any they were to keep them alive and tag them with the small GPS trackers he had provided. Had he not watched the poachers' encounter with the wild man first-hand, he would never have believed it. Obviously the poachers had thought no man or beast could resist the might of a heavily armed gang – a mistake they had paid for with their lives. But still, they did successfully plant a GPS tracker on the wild man before he mercilessly slew them.

Following the white ape was proving more difficult than anticipated. He couldn't believe any creature could pass through the dense forest at such speed. He had been forced to push ahead of Paulvitch just so he could make it to the plateau before nightfall. Now here he was, lying flat in thick mud.

Patience was the single virtue Rokoff possessed. It was the key quality for any hunter. He'd counted thirteen targets. Tarzan's distinctive thermal pattern made him stand out from the gorillas. The wild man crouched next to the large silverback. Both of them tilted their heads trying to pick up the faintest hint of what lay in the darkness. Rokoff was certain he hadn't made a sound, but still something had alerted them.

With a single slow deliberate movement, Rokoff switched his night-vision goggles from thermal imaging to infrared. He blinked as his eyes adjusted to the glowing grey-green wash of the plateau. Even though the storm clouds blotted out the moon, the goggles amplified enough ambient light to reproduce the lighting levels of a full moon. The monochrome colour palette occasionally made his targets blend into the background, but when they moved it provided the perfect tool for night combat.

The wild man's head suddenly turned in his direction. Rokoff saw the pale eyes peer at him, luminous like a cat's in the night vision. Rokoff's finger froze on the button he had just pressed. Surely the apeman couldn't have heard the sound? The equipment was designed to be virtually silent and Rokoff himself hadn't heard anything. Yet the wild man half turned towards him, his head bobbed as if trying to detect a subtle odour. Rokoff knew he was well concealed, but he experienced a sudden doubt. Could the wild man see him in the darkness? Had life in the jungle sharpened his senses to an extraordinary, almost superhuman, level?

The silverback grunted again and the wild man's attention slid from Rokoff to the darkness across the plateau. Rokoff quickly checked the position of the other gorillas, all sheltering under the jungle canopy.

When he looked back at the rock he saw only the silverback. The wild man had vanished.

Rokoff felt something he had not experienced during a hunt since he was a teenager. Panic. Had he been spotted? He scanned the plateau, his head turning so fast he almost struck a tree and gave away his position. There was no sign of the ape-man, but Rokoff hadn't become a great hunter by assuming his prey was weaker than him. Every animal had guile enough to be respected; this opponent doubly so. He switched the goggles back to thermal imaging, half expecting to see the deadly figure of a man standing over him.

Instead, the warm hues of the gorillas revealed themselves and with these a faint thermal image of a figure leaping through the tree canopy impossibly fast and, more importantly, away from Rokoff.

Whatever had spooked the wild man was a blessing and he was thankful for the distraction. Rokoff turned his attention back to the aircraft and wondered what secrets it held, but forced such ideas from his head. He was a man with little room in his mind for anything other than planning the outcome of the hunt. Okeke had placed a very specific order with his top hunter, and Rokoff had to deliver on it.

He picked up the thermal image of the baby gorilla sitting within the torn aircraft fuselage. With slow, deliberate movements, Rokoff slid his hunting rifle from his shoulder and lined up the young ape in his crosshairs.

11

Robbie had struggled to keep up with Jane as she led him along the animal trail, warily checking for any new poacher traps. The beams from their wind-up torches shone across the Dum-Dum clearing. Jane beat against a hollow tree and Robbie was surprised by the deep timbre of the sound that rang out. They stood in the rain and waited in silence for what seemed like an eternity before Tarzan appeared. Jane stumbled over her words as she tried to explain the threat Rokoff posed. Concerned for his family, Tarzan took Jane with him. The only words he grunted to Robbie were about following the trail back to the camp and waiting.

Now Robbie sat in Rokoff's Land Cruiser to shelter from the rain and decide on what he should do. His nervous fingers toyed with the GPS scanner, which still flashed the location of the discarded tag in the mud. He randomly pressed some of the buttons and flicked through different channel frequencies – stopping on one that was rapidly moving away from him. Tarzan – it had to be. Nothing else could move so swiftly, but he couldn't guess how Rokoff had managed to tag him.

His heart was in his mouth when the blip stopped for some time. They had been gone for almost an hour and a half so they must have reached Tarzan's home. Could they be at the lost aircraft? He stared at the longitude and latitude figures, burning them into his memory. This is what they needed. He headed to the bar debating if this was the right time to tell Clark. Most of the loggers had gone to their shacks for the night leaving only Mister David and Esmée sitting with Clark and Archie. They were discussing the possibility of moving the camp once more to a new area of rare hardwoods their scouts had discovered. They were so wrapped in their conversation that they didn't notice him enter.

'We can get the next boatload through to Nigeria,' said Clark pointing to some figures written on a paper. 'Get the timber laundered there and we get a damn good price.'

Robbie glanced at the scanner and saw that Tarzan was now moving back in their direction. This was not the time to tell Clark. Lost in thought, he stumbled into a table with a loud clatter. All eyes turned to him. He must have been a sight – drenched to the skin, covered in mud and clutching the GPS.

'What's up?' said Clark, automatically suspicious.

Robbie hesitated then told them what they'd found out about Rokoff, and about their warnings to Tarzan. He saw Archie's hand massage his temples when he told them how Jane had left with the ape-man, but quickly assured him that they were on their way back.

They all hurried out in the rain to search through Rokoff's belongings. The equipment in the Land Cruiser was state-of-the-art; some of it was even still in its original packaging. Clark opened a long case, revealing a brand-new hunting rifle.

'Well, he ain't taggin' no apes with this thing. It'd blow a head clean off the shoulders.'

'Why leave it all here?' asked Robbie.

'If he's a contract hunter, then I bet this was all given to him as part of the deal. Car'll be a rental. He can afford to leave it behind.'

Almost two hours later Tarzan and Jane returned to the camp and things moved from bad to worse.

Jane was pale and taciturn. Tarzan was in a volcanic rage. He marched past Archie and the others and immediately set upon Rokoff's Land Cruiser. Robbie watched, stunned, as Tarzan began sniffing everything, like a bloodhound. He started opening cases and tossing them into the mud. It wasn't long before he was bellowing with rage and smashed a case through the windscreen. He tore the passenger seat from the bolts in the floor and hurled it at the driver's door with such force that it took the door clean off its hinges. Then, still in a wild fury, Tarzan climbed on to the roof and howled to the rain with a cry more savage than anything Robbie had ever heard. Tarzan's fists pounded into the reinforced steel roof until his knuckles bled and he punched a hole through the metal. His wild tantrum seemed to quell and he leaped down, heading straight for Archie.

Clark's hand instinctively went for the pistol he always kept holstered to his thigh, but Mister David quickly reached out to stop him. A move that probably saved his life.

Tarzan glowered at Archie who took an involuntary step back.

'You bring this on Tarzan!' he growled.

'I had no idea who Rokoff was, I swear.'

Robbie was convinced Tarzan was about to strike Archie and he wondered how long it would take for him to reveal it was he, Robbie, who had brought Rokoff into the camp.

'He's telling the truth!' said Jane, suddenly positioning herself in front of Tarzan.

Panic crossed Archie's face and Clark tensed as if

Jane had just stepped in front of a lion, but she didn't seem afraid and, to their amazement, Tarzan backed down.

'Rokoff has taken Karnath,' explained Jane.

Archie looked confused. 'What's Karnath?'

'Karnath is a young gorilla,' Robbie explained.

'Killed him?' said Esmée with a gasp, her hand covering her mouth in horror. She had lived through many hardships in the Congo, but had been brought up to respect the gorillas, which were a symbol of hope in her country.

'No. Not dead,' said Tarzan. 'Kid-napped.' The word was thick on his tongue, and Robbie guessed it was a term Jane had just taught him.

'Why would he do that?' asked Robbie.

'Pet trade, circus, third-world zoo. Could be any-thin',' said Clark, a little too knowledgeably. 'People offer a good price for exotic pets.'

The grief on Tarzan's face deepened and Jane was visibly shaken by Clark's cold analysis.

'Tarzan,' said Archie hesitantly, 'please, believe us. We would never have allowed Rokoff to come here if we'd known.'

Robbie was expecting an explosive response from Tarzan – another display of unbridled rage. Instead, the ape-man lowered his head, looked askance at Archie and said nothing. The simple action brought silence to the camp, broken only by the constant rain. When Tarzan spoke, his voice was uncharacteristically subdued.

'Archie destroy Tarzan's land. Bring pain to Tarzan's family.'

'We'll do everything we can to help,' said Archie who, like everybody else, was nervous about where the conversation was going.

Tarzan spoke in a low voice, and he appeared to struggle with each word. 'Tarzan find Karnath. Bring him home.'

'I'm coming with you,' said Jane almost immediately.

Robbie watched Archie's hands clench into fists and the veins in the side of his neck begin to throb. He stared at Jane as if willing her to retract the words, but said nothing. To his relief Tarzan spoke up.

'No. Rokoff hunter. Dangerous.'

'You're safer here,' Archie told Jane, thankful for Tarzan's support.

'No way!' said Jane defiantly. She spun round to face Tarzan, angry with his dismissal. 'I'm coming with you. Rokoff is a modern guy, he's not a jungle animal. He's more advanced than you. He's got guns, GPS maps, technology that allows him to see in the dark – have you? If he's heading out of the jungle then you're going to need all the back-up you can get. And when my family was taken,' she indicated the loggers with a sweeping finger, 'you helped me get them back. I owe you.'

Tarzan nodded. Robbie suddenly felt Archie and Clark looking at him. Clark's eyes narrowed a little, prompting him to step up.

'I'll come too,' said Robbie. Jane looked unsure so he continued to justify his offer. 'Like you said, Tarzan came back for us.' Tarzan's intense gaze fell on Robbie. The suspicion and anger had transformed into a questioning look.

'Robbie come,' said Tarzan nodding his head. Robbie was shocked when Tarzan clapped a strong hand on his shoulder and was equally surprised by the next comment. 'Robbie help kill Rokoff.'

'K-kill?' stammered Robbie. 'Let's just figure out how to get Karnath back, OK?'

'Do we leave now?' Jane asked.

Tarzan shook his head. 'Dark not good to hunt. We leave when sun rise.'

★

With some difficulty, Robbie and Jane finally managed to get Tarzan to check for the GPS tracker the poachers had planted on him. Since his only item of clothing was a torn and grubby pair of cargo shorts it wasn't long before he found it lodged in a pocket.

Robbie destroyed the tracker by smashing it between a pair of rocks.

Tarzan wouldn't accept anything from the camp. He didn't shelter in any of the shacks and he pawed at the hot food Esmée brought him and refused to eat it. He lifted a chunk of meat from the stew and eyed it with disgust.

'Why burn meat?'

'That's how you're supposed to eat it,' said Esmée. But no amount of explanation of the merits of cooked food could convince Tarzan.

Instead, Tarzan disappeared into the jungle to rest. Jane slept fitfully, running events over in her mind. She had expected her father to reprimand her for volunteering to leave with Tarzan, but he had said nothing.

Robbie couldn't sleep at all. Before they'd turned in he'd managed to snatch a quick conversation with Clark. Clark had purchased a palm-sized camcorder during their last big supply run. He was planning to acquire video evidence of Tarzan and the aircraft, and this trip would be the perfect opportunity for Robbie to get it. The device was waterproof and discreet enough to be stashed in the deep pocket of his combat trousers. It would be best, he thought, to keep Jane unaware of his intentions.

A further search of Rokoff's Land Cruiser revealed

several more GPS trackers, heavy-duty wind-up torches, climbing ropes, field provisions and medical supplies – everything needed for a long-haul expedition. Archie charged Robbie's satellite phone and made him swear he would keep in touch about their progress. Robbie was surprised that Archie hadn't demanded reassurances over his daughter's safety, but it was clear that he trusted Tarzan's jungle survival skills.

Dawn chased the storm clouds away, revealing a pale blue sky. Weighed down with full backpacks, Robbie and Jane waited beside Rokoff's vehicle. Robbie idly flicked the blade of his machete through the mud, carving out random patterns. He asked for a gun, but Clark refused to give him one.

'You don't want blood on your hands, boy,' Clark had warned. 'Leave that to Tarzan.'

Again, Robbie wondered just how much Clark had dug into his past. He had wanted the gun for self-defence against deadly jungle creatures, not to use against the Russian.

Robbie and Jane waited in silence. He couldn't see anybody else, but suspected Archie was watching them from one of the cabins. Eventually, Tarzan emerged from the jungle, looking solemn.

'Now we hunt.'

The cold statement suddenly made Robbie realise what he was about to get himself into.

This wasn't a rescue mission. This was revenge.

They hurried to keep up with Tarzan as they travelled through the jungle. Robbie had seen how Tarzan carried Jane through the trees, but as the two of them were weighed down with equipment, that was impossible now. Instead, Tarzan would take to the trees to scout ahead then return to encourage them on. The journey was uneventful. Robbie didn't know if Tarzan was clearing dangers from their path or if animals just instinctively avoided the wild man.

After hours of exhausting trekking the sun was high in the sky and the humidity had risen, sucking Robbie's strength with every step until his legs began to shake. He was impressed at how Jane kept ahead of him, never once complaining. She'd changed so much from the bratty girl he had first met.

'I need to stop,' said Robbie sitting on a fallen log. He expected Tarzan to complain, but he just nodded and then vanished up a tree. 'Man of few words,' Robbie muttered before taking a long swig from his water canteen. Suddenly, a deep howling from above almost made him choke. It was answered immediately by a trumpeting sound Robbie recognised.

With a loud crack the trees suddenly parted and a fully-grown jungle elephant stepped on to the trail.

It was Tantor, Tarzan's companion, who had led his herd to help save Robbie when the jungle rebel Tafari had kidnapped him. Of all the animals, Robbie was most enchanted with being so close to the elephant. Tantor trumpeted loudly, curling his trunk over his head in greeting. Tarzan patted the animal's rough, hairy flank then gestured to Robbie and Jane.

'Ride.'

Far from a sedate stroll through the jungle on Tantor's back, Robbie and Jane were rewarded with a terrifying race through the undergrowth. Tantor followed snaking trails at a brisk trot that almost shook Robbie from his seat on the back of the elephant's neck. Jane clung on to him from behind and Tarzan leaped from the branches high overhead, free running from limb to limb, criss-crossing the trail ahead.

Many times Robbie was forced to duck as the branches whipped too close for comfort and he was convinced it was only a matter of time before he was thrown off.

Tantor was driven forward by Tarzan's urgency and the elephant's pace never ceased, even when the trail started climbing up the gentle mountain slopes. After another few hours they reached a plateau which offered a spectacular view over a stretch of jungle that split into two valleys. They could clearly see several rivers down below; brown stains meandering through the green hillsides.

'Is this where you live?' asked Robbie, trying to keep the excitement from his voice as he and Jane climbed down from Tantor.

'No,' said Tarzan. Robbie was disappointed, but tried to hide it. 'Karnath somewhere there in danger.'

A troubled look passed Tarzan's face at the thought of the little gorilla.

'Rokoff come this way,' said Tarzan, indicating to the valleys below.

'He could be anywhere.' Robbie remembered how hopeless he had felt following Jane when she had been lost out here. 'How are we supposed to find him?'

'Maybe he tried to go back to the camp to drive out?' suggested Jane.

Tarzan shook his head. 'Hunter will leave with prey. Rokoff will not return.'

'If it was me taking Karnath,' said Robbie, ignoring the sharp look Tarzan gave him, 'and I wanted to leave unseen, then I would head straight for the nearest river. Problem is, we have two to choose from.'

Tarzan regarded Robbie thoughtfully, then nodded his approval. The idea obviously hadn't occurred to him. Tarzan crouched on the ledge of the cliff top, his eyes squinting against the sun. For several minutes he didn't move.

'We can't just wait,' said Jane in frustration. 'Every minute we waste, Rokoff's getting further away.' Tarzan didn't seem to hear. 'Tarzan? Are you listening to me?'

Tantor suddenly brayed, shifting nervously as he sensed something in the jungle – then Sheeta landed gracefully next to Robbie. He froze; being so close to the big cat still unnerved him. Jane displayed no such qualms and ran over to Sheeta, ruffling a hand over his smooth fur.

'Sheeta! Good boy!!'

She could have been talking to a pet dog. To Robbie's amazement, the panther issued a grumbling purr and rubbed the side of his head against her leg, circling playfully around her. Tarzan quickly brought the reunion back to earth.

'Sheeta!'

The cat crossed to Tarzan's side and dropped something he had been carrying. It was a fragment of cloth from a backpack, the same colour as the ones the Russians carried.

'Go!' Tarzan commanded. Sheeta bounded along the cliff top, and gave a quick glance behind to check Tarzan was following, before disappearing into the undergrowth. Robbie hoped they could accompany them on Tantor, but when he looked around the elephant had silently vanished back into the jungle.

Robbie and Jane quickly went after Tarzan but were immediately slowed down by the dense foliage, which Robbie hacked aside with his machete. Sheeta speeded ahead and Tarzan took to the trees. They eventually made up ground on the steep mountain slope, though they lost sight of Tarzan several times. Once he was gone for almost an hour, but Jane insisted they push ahead, convinced that Tarzan would come back if they were lost. Robbie didn't share her level of trust, but each time he started to doubt, Tarzan would appear just ahead, hunched on a branch waiting for them.

Jane never once complained but Robbie was starting to feel weak.

'How much further? I'm exhausted!'

Tarzan answered by throwing something at Robbie. Then he leaped down, and shoved a green papaya-like fruit in his hands. 'Eat!'

Robbie hesitated and only took a bite when he saw Jane eagerly crunch into one. The orange flesh inside was sweet and textured like a melon's. The taste was unlike anything he'd eaten before. No sooner had he devoured it than he felt a surge of energy course through him, shaking all fatigue away.

Whatever it was it was a perfect natural remedy. He ate another, stashing several more in his backpack.

'Any sign of Rokoff?'

Tarzan led them down a steep trail where the trees suddenly cleared and they found themselves on the sandy bank of a wide river. Sheeta was already there, lapping water as he kept an alert eye out for danger. Tarzan pointed to a circle of charcoal, the remains of a campfire.

'Are you sure this was Rokoff?' asked Jane. 'There are poachers, loggers . . . all kinds of people hiding out here.'

Robbie knelt by the ashes and poked them with a stick, revealing several plastic ration packs, which had only been partially burned. He lifted a can up. The label was barely legible but he could see a date penned on the side, in the same place Esmée always wrote when stocking the inventory.

'I'm pretty sure it's Rokoff's mess. This is from our camp.'

Tarzan clapped Robbie on the back, so hard that it knocked the breath out of him.

'Robbie make good hunter.'

Robbie was surprised by the compliment. Tarzan moved to the water's edge and traced a finger over a stretch of flattened sand.

'Rokoff take boat from here.' The sand was

flattened diagonally into the river, indicating they had launched downstream.

'That's just great,' sighed Jane. 'How're we going to catch up now? We can't swim after them.'

'But we can make a raft,' Robbie suggested. 'We float the logs downstream all the time so why should it be any different?' He walked to the water's edge and tossed a stone in.

'Robbie . . .' said Tarzan.

'Looks very deep—'

The calm river in front of him suddenly exploded in a mass of white water. Robbie felt time slow down as an enormous pair of jagged jaws punctured through the rising curtain of water – ready to snap him in half.

12

Paulvitch coughed as he inhaled the sickly cigarette fumes puffing around Rokoff's head.

'Do you have to smoke that rubbish in here?' Paulvitch protested.

Rokoff gave him an icy stare then deliberately blew streams of smoke directly at him, sending him into another coughing fit.

'I'm going to be sick,' snapped Paulvitch, using the cuff of his sleeve to wipe the beads of sweat running down his temples. He had been complaining constantly since they boarded the boat. The stifling atmosphere in the cabin did nothing to relieve his condition.

Rokoff closed his eyes and tried to blank the man out. It wasn't easy. If Paulvitch wasn't moaning he was making hacking noises in the back of his throat. A small CD player whirled through a Tchaikovsky compilation. The music always buoyed Rokoff's spirits after a particularly arduous adventure, but it was difficult to concentrate with Paulvitch's whining and the dull thrum of the boat's engines. Not that this had been a difficult job. All the pieces of his plan had fallen into place without incident, except for the violent demise of the local poachers he had hired, which had not only saved him money (if they were dead, he didn't have to pay them), but also given him a first-hand glimpse of one of the most lethal creatures on earth.

Taking a rare mountain gorilla would have been a big achievement for most poachers, but for the Russian it barely registered. As a child, Rokoff became a skilled hunter in the Siberian plains, but back then he hunted out of necessity for food and skins rather than pleasure. He had pushed himself in the wilderness. Living on the edge sharpened his survival skills and developed his desire to explore the world. His school education brought with it increasing disappointment that the world had already been thoroughly explored. There were no dark places on the map, no civilisations still waiting to be discovered. But he clung on to the hope that the tales of unknown creatures and hidden subterranean worlds he'd read about really existed.

His craving for the impossible hunt was something that gnawed at him with every waking moment. As a young man he learned to pilot various aircraft just so he could search for the Yeti high in the Himalayas and the flying Ropen in Papua New Guinea. But these proved to be futile adventures that eroded his belief in the unknown. They had turned him into a bitter man, angry that the stories which had captured his childhood imagination were nothing more than fiction.

Now he had found something really incredible; something he had only heard about in legend. The white ape. A wild man – a hunter with a survival acumen greater than his own. The ultimate prey – the ultimate challenge. Rokoff smiled to himself. The hunt was just beginning.

The scratched Tchaikovsky CD jumped and glitched, bringing Rokoff back to Paulvitch's complaining.

'We should make Okeke pay double for dragging us to this sweatbox,' he grumbled.

Rokoff stubbed out his cigarette and stood up, mopping his brow with a carefully folded handkerchief plucked from the breast pocket of his cream linen suit.

'You possess a terrible lack of imagination, Alexis,' he said.

'And you have too much.'

'Perhaps. But which will be our undoing?'

Paulvitch scowled. He hated Rokoff talking down to him, something he did on a regular basis. He didn't reply. Instead he sat hunched forward in his chair, propping his head in his hands and hoping he wouldn't be sick again. Rokoff took his panama hat from the table and used it to fan himself as he left the cabin.

*

The ship's hold was oppressively hot, and the drum of the engines echoed in the wide space. Rokoff's hunting equipment was stored in one corner. Aside from his trusted Saiga rifle the rest of it was easy to replace. He had decided not to return to the logging camp because of the girl's connection with the apes. Getting the young gorilla out of the jungle was his immediate priority and he suspected the loggers would have tried to stop him.

He knelt in front of the cage pushed against one wall. Karnath was slumped in the corner. The little ape's brown eyes flickered wide with fear when he saw Rokoff, a reaction the Russian approved of.

'How are you, my little friend?'

Karnath had only experienced life around the other gorillas in his troop and responded with a verbal cue they used to communicate. He grunted, waiting for Rokoff to do the same back, indicating everything would be OK. Rokoff merely grinned, showing too many teeth. Karnath took the eye contact as a threat and looked away. His mind was still fogged from the tranquilliser dart Rokoff had shot into him.

'Wake up!' Rokoff thumped the cage hard, startling Karnath.

Karnath whimpered in fright. Rokoff hit the cage again, harder this time. The little gorilla tried to push himself further into the corner of the cage as Rokoff struck the bars for a third time.

'That's waking you up now, eh? You need to be lively for your new owner or I'll have to throw you into the river and find myself a new pet.' Rokoff enjoyed watching the fear in Karnath's eyes. 'You don't want to put me through all that trouble again, do you?'

Karnath was used to fresh air, greenery and freedom, but now he clamped his tiny hand over his face to block out the cold steel and acrid fumes from the boat's diesel engines. Being far from anything comforting and familiar, he was more terrified than he had ever been.

★

Sheer instinct saved Robbie from the attack. He jumped aside, falling to the sand. Water drenched him as the mouth tore into his backpack. The Nile crocodile's more than two hundred kilo bulk slammed to the ground next to him.

The attack had been so sudden that Robbie was in a state of shock. For a split second he thought he was safe. Then the huge reptile rapidly backed into the water taking his backpack with it. The beast's immense jaws had almost severed the pack in half, breaking one strap – but Robbie's arm was still hooked through the other one.

He yelled in terror as he was pulled backwards into the river. He reached for Jane as she lunged for him. Their fingers locked – and then she was yanked to the floor and dragged across the sand until her grip slipped.

Robbie heard his name being screamed just as the frothing river closed over his head. He managed to suck in a lungful of air before water filled his mouth.

The next few seconds were a confused jumble. he felt the backpack tear from his shoulder and he was free. Frantically, he thrashed towards the surface, breaking the water metres from the riverbank. He sank into mud and was relieved that the water only came up to his waist. He saw Jane and Sheeta on the bank staring at him – no, not *at* him, but *behind* him.

Robbie twisted around to see Tarzan straddling the thrashing crocodile. He had one arm around the beast's throat; his other easily pushed the animal's elongated snout closed.

The reptile flexed and twisted, trying to throw Tarzan off. Its tail skimmed across the water forcing Robbie to duck to avoid having his head knocked off. He didn't realise how big the crocodile was until it arced back into the water, taking Tarzan with it.

Robbie scrambled to the bank, falling to his knees as Jane ran to him, her gaze firmly fixed on where Tarzan had vanished. She opened her mouth to call his name – just as the crocodile darted out of the river, straight for them.

Robbie stood and pulled Jane with him as they ran in a zigzag. The animal was incredibly fast in a straight line, but, as they recalled from Esmée's lectures, it had difficulty following their constantly changing path. Robbie lost his grip on Jane as she darted to the left.

Sheeta streaked ahead. It was the first time Robbie had ever seen the panther frightened. He glanced back to see that Jane had fallen behind. The crocodile's tooth-filled jaws opened either side of her legs.

'Watch out!'

Tarzan shot from the water and grabbed the reptile's tail, every muscle in his body tensing as he braced himself in the river's mud. The crocodile was pulled to a dead stop. Tarzan heaved it backwards as the jaws sliced closed – slamming together a centimetre from Jane's legs.

Robbie watched in astonishment as Tarzan hauled the animal back into the water. The reptile violently writhed until it freed itself from his grip, but rather than turn and attack, it quickly headed for deeper water, sinking beneath the surface without a ripple.

Tarzan waded ashore, his ripped shorts soaked. Blood trickled from a cut on his leg inflicted by the crocodile's hind claws. He was breathing heavily, exhausted from the struggle. He cast a critical eye over Robbie and Jane to check they were unharmed. Once satisfied, he rapidly shook his head to dislodge the water in his ears and looked back to the river.

'Now Robbie build boat,' he said, as if nothing had happened.

★

They continued working as the sun began to set, chopping down small trees to build the raft until their clothes were damp with sweat, but after the crocodile attack, neither Jane nor Robbie dared to take a dip in the river to cool down. Felling trees with the machete was a laborious process. Tarzan watched, fascinated, as Robbie lashed the trunks together with the rope they had salvaged from his torn backpack.

Tarzan left briefly to find food, leaving Sheeta to

watch over them. The panther kept high in the trees, but his presence put Robbie on edge rather than reassuring him. Without Tarzan around, it was just another wild animal.

'I can't believe we're doing this for a stupid monkey,' he grumbled, which provoked an icy look from Jane.

Later, taking a break, Jane talked quietly with Tarzan at the river's edge. Robbie caught enough of the conversation to know that Jane was telling him about the Greystokes. Tarzan was clearly unimpressed.

Robbie checked the camcorder in his pocket. Luckily it was waterproof and still worked. He managed to sneak in several shots of Tarzan, carefully zooming in on his face to get his profile just as Clark had instructed. By studying photos of the Greystokes online, they'd found that Tarzan strikingly resembled his father in appearance. Robbie knew this alone was not proof enough, but it was helpful. Videoing the aircraft would be the indisputable evidence.

In the dying rays of the sun they cast their vessel out into the river. It was broad, flat and big enough to carry the three humans, but the gaps between the logs made it look as though it was already falling apart. Robbie fastened hollow bamboo strips across the deck, trapping air to keep it afloat, and made a pair of basic oars from a dead tree.

'We're ready to go at dawn,' said Robbie, although he was struggling to see how they could make up the time to catch Rokoff.

'No. Go now,' stated Tarzan with his usual directness. He started to push the raft into the water, but Robbie put his foot on it to stop him.

'Wait a second, we can't navigate the river at night. We don't know what's out there!'

'Out there? Rocks, *gimla*, difficult places for boat to cross.'

'Exactly.'

'Rokoff must stop. We catch up.'

Tarzan tilted the raft to dislodge Robbie's foot and pushed it out. It dipped in the water, but remained afloat.

'How're we going to see where we're going?'

Jane held up the last of the wind-up torches they had brought; she had been unable to locate the one that had fallen from Robbie's pack.

'With this.' She smiled at Robbie, pleased with her foresight. Robbie was too tired to return the smile.

★

The voyage down the river proved to be less terrifying than Robbie had anticipated. The pale moon shone down the meandering river's path and Jane at the front sat facing forward, sweeping the torch beam ahead to reveal any immediate hidden dangers. Sheeta had disappeared into the jungle when they set out; Robbie was relieved Tarzan didn't attempt to bring the cat on board too.

Robbie and Tarzan pulled on the oars, and they caught a strong current in the middle of the river that bore them silently on. Occasionally Jane warned of rocks ahead and they steered around them without incident.

Their fatigue played tricks on their eyes in the semi-darkness. Shapes loomed out of the water and several times Robbie panicked when he thought he saw a crocodile. Most turned out to be floating driftwood while others simply vanished into the gloom.

Hours passed in silence and Robbie's arms were almost numb from rowing. He begged to rest and Tarzan reluctantly agreed. The raft continued onwards caught by the strong current, and Tarzan used his oar as a rudder to round each sweeping turn. Without the steady churn of the oars, other sounds floated towards them across the river. Splashes that were uncomfortably close, the constant chirping of frogs, insects and the occasional screeches of animals Robbie and Jane could not identify. Hungry eyes in the ominous wall of dark trees along the river reflected from Jane's torch beam.

Once Robbie had rested, he took up the oar again

to speed them along. He wondered how far away Rokoff was and, even with Tarzan pushing them on, he doubted they could ever catch up. None of them knew how long they would be on Rokoff's trail. It could be days or even weeks. Compared with what little they had with them on the raft, Karibu Mji was starting to resemble a luxury resort.

Suddenly, Jane screamed. A large shape suddenly loomed in the water. Another appeared alongside. Robbie thought they were hippos and immediately lifted his oar to strike them. A cross hippopotamus could easily smash their raft apart and was deadlier than a hungry crocodile.

Tarzan's hand shot out and pulled the oar from Robbie's hand before he could bring it down.

'No!' said Tarzan. 'Friend. Look.'

The creatures looked like a cross between a small hippo and a seal. Robbie and Jane could see flippers in the murky water, propelling the animals to thick clumps of floating vegetation. They would occasionally dip beneath the surface, revealing broad, shovel-like tails.

'Manatees!' exclaimed Jane. 'Can I touch them?' she asked. Tarzan nodded encouragingly and Jane reached out a hand tentatively.

Robbie followed her lead and was surprised to feel soft wrinkly skin. The manatees didn't appear to be bothered by their contact and continued swimming around the raft until they'd eaten the vegetation, before silently submerging under the black water.

Jane offered to take over rowing from Robbie for a while, and they switched places on the raft. It rocked alarmingly with the sudden shift in weight as Robbie sat down at the front, but then quickly levelled out once again.

Robbie cast the torch beam across the water and felt his eyes growing heavy. Behind him, Jane started talking to Tarzan, a continuation of a conversation they'd been having for a while.

'Are you sure you don't want to know anything about your family in England?' she said in a low voice.

'Karnath family,' said Tarzan softly.

'What about D'Arnot? The Greystokes thought he was lying. I read that they even tried to have him arrested.' Tarzan never met her gaze when she spoke about the Frenchman. She could see the loss of his friend still hurt. 'I think D'Arnot thought you were better off here.' She fell into a thoughtful silence before continuing. 'And you know what? I'm starting to agree. I don't know if the outside world is ready for you.'

While eavesdropping, Robbie was not paying attention to what lay ahead. Just then, something struck the raft with such force they were almost hurled into the water and they all cried out in alarm. Robbie's torch was flung from his hand and skittered across the deck. They grabbed on to the trunks as the wood began to crack. Now they saw a huge floating branch, about the size of a jeep, tearing through the raft, splitting the bound timbers in a V-shape. Ropes snapped and the strong river current pivoted the raft around the sturdy limb, cracking more wood. The raft split apart under Robbie's backside, and he hurled himself to one side.

The current forced the raft to twist and the front corner rose from the water as it became wedged on the branch. Robbie's torch fell between the timbers as, with a final terrible cracking noise, the raft was torn in two.

Jane and Tarzan fell into the water but clung on to their half of the raft. Jane's backpack slid off the deck, but one strap got caught on a broken bamboo spar, saving it from sinking.

Robbie's half of the raft was tangled on the stump and broke apart as the current twisted it. Robbie wrapped himself around the massive tree branch, determined not to fall in the river for a second time as the remains of his shattered raft were swept away beneath him.

Strengthening his grip on the branch, Robbie

looked around. Cloud partly covered the moon, but there was enough pale light to see that he was in the middle of the wide river and could just make out two figures in the water far ahead. He heard Jane call out, but her voice was faint as the fragment of raft they clung to spiralled away from him.

'The boat!'

What boat? Robbie recoiled as something brushed past his waterlogged boots. He lifted his legs higher over the water.

Then lights slowly came into focus as his branch drifted around a sharp crook in the river. The lights outlined the deck of a rusty old freighter moored to the riverbank.

Black smoke issued from the boat's funnel and Robbie could see figures standing on the stern deck. From this distance it was too dark for them to see him, but he knew that it was only a matter of time before he was spotted. Judging from the rifles slung over their shoulders, it could be Rokoff's boat and, if so, he was certain bullets would start flying.

13

'*Glupyî!*' snarled Paulvitch, as the satellite dish clattered to the deck. He smacked the Congolese crewman across the ear. The man was a head taller than the wiry Russian, but did not retaliate. The crew had already been on the receiving end of Paulvitch's temper and there was now an atmosphere of tension on board the vessel.

The crewman obediently set the satellite receiver upright and angled the dish as he had been instructed until an indicator light on the back turned green.

'Move,' snapped Paulvitch, pushing the man roughly aside. Paulvitch was a bully, but he in turn was treated badly by Rokoff. As harsh as his boss was, Paulvitch didn't want to lose this or the next job – the money was good, and he loved being paid to shoot things. So instead he vented his frustrations on the crew.

He connected his laptop to the satellite dish and

selected the images he had taken of the little ape. Whatever Rokoff had done to the gorilla had left it shaking and frightened when Paulvitch approached with his camera. But he still managed to take a few good shots. Okeke wanted evidence his prize was in mint condition and Paulvitch didn't relish the idea of going back to the jungle to take a healthier specimen.

The satellite transmission was slow, and Paulvitch impatiently watched the progress bar creep towards completion as he slapped mosquitoes whining around his neck. Then a dull thump on the hull caught his attention. He peered curiously over the rail and gazed into the dark water. It was impossible to see anything clearly but he could have sworn there was something near the prow. He listened intently, then heard another clunk against the metal.

'Give me your torch,' he growled at the crewman. 'Now!'

The crewman unclipped the torch hooked to his belt and Paulvitch snatched it, shining the beam down the side of the boat. A large log was tangled in the anchor chain and the eddying current swung it against the hull. It wasn't damaging the ship, so it wasn't his problem. He tossed the torch back at the crewman, smirking when it struck the unprepared man in the chest. Paulvitch turned back to his laptop.

Just above the waterline, Robbie clung to the anchor chain. He had tried to climb the links but his wet boots kept slipping off. He was desperate not to attract attention from the deck, but then he slipped again, banging his head against the hull, and almost falling into the river. Looking up, he saw a head appear over the railings. Holding tightly to the chain, he sank to his chest in the water, willing the shadows to conceal him. He held his breath as torchlight swept over the river. Were large shapes moving through the water around his feet? Or was it just his mind playing tricks? He dreaded to think what lethal creatures might be swimming around him.

Something nudged his foot – it was a solid object and definitely alive. The light disappeared from the deck and he heard Paulvitch walking away. It was all the motivation he needed to hoist himself from the water. He climbed up the anchor chain, covering several decks. Luckily the hawse through which the chain passed was neglected and rusted chunks had fallen away over the years, creating a hole just large enough for Robbie to clamber on deck.

The anchor chain coiled around a large capstan on the deck, which Robbie ducked behind for cover as he peered down the length of the ship. Near the stern he spotted Paulvitch crouched over a laptop and satellite dish, with a muscular crewman standing close by.

Between them the flat deck was broken only by a huge pair of closed hatch doors which led to the hold below. Robbie guessed that was where he'd find the kidnapped ape.

The rest of the boat was quiet, but Robbie was cautious. For a vessel this size, he reckoned there would be at least a fifteen-man strong crew somewhere below deck. The boat's bridge was dark, and he could see no other lights from any cabins on the deck. All he had to do was wait until the Russian went inside and he would then be free to sneak around. He had successfully stowed away on a busy freighter across the Atlantic, so he didn't see the riverboat as a challenge.

After a great deal of swearing, Paulvitch clouted the other man across the chest with his laptop then stormed inside leaving the snarling crewman to carry the portable dish after him. Robbie waited to check that Paulvitch didn't double back, then he sneaked across the deck to the hold doors.

The doors were fastened with new chains and a padlock bound them together, foiling Robbie's plan to break in and rescue Karnath. He would have to go down into the boat to access the hold. He looked around, half hoping to see Tarzan loom from the shadows, but there was no sign of him. He started worrying about Jane, but shook the thought from his head. He knew she would be safe.

He crept towards the door in the bulkhead that Paulvitch had disappeared through. It was partially open, beckoning him inside.

Stale, hot air hit Robbie as he entered the corridor. The cream paintwork peeled from the walls like a rash, lights flickered erratically and he could hear the dull throb of the engine vibrating through the floor. Another corridor crossed up ahead at right angles and Robbie cautiously peered around the corner. There was no sign of where Paulvitch had gone. He began to feel uneasy; he had no desire to run into the boat's crew. Working on a freighter like this, in the heart of the Congo, attracted only hard-nosed cut-throat men.

A nearby door was held open on a metal catch and beyond it a stairway ran down to the deck below. He slowly climbed down it, more than aware that his boots squelched with every step.

On the lower deck he listened intently; again, nothing but the thrum of the engines. He reckoned there was one more floor before he could enter the hold. A short corridor ran off from the main one and another companionway led down. He carefully descended to the next deck. Here, heavy pipes were bolted to the ceiling with a snarl of electrical cables running between them. It was hotter than outside and the noise from the engines was even louder.

Robbie headed in the opposite direction from the engines. The hatchway ahead was closed. He strained to turn the locking wheel. With both hands and all his strength he managed to turn the rusted mechanism and shoulder the door open.

The air in the darkness beyond was stiflingly hot. Robbie's eyes refused to adjust to the blackness and he groped for a light switch around the door. He found one and received a biting shock as his wet hands flicked it on. He sucked in his breath to stop yelling aloud in pain.

A single fluorescent tube blinked into life – revealing a small cage against one wall. Robbie slowly walked towards it. At first he thought it was empty, until Karnath moved inside, the ape's black fur blending him into the shadows.

Robbie knelt down and Karnath's sensitive brown eyes met his own. The look of fear in the gorilla's face was almost human. Its entire body shook with fright. Images of finding his sister, Sophie, flashed into Robbie's mind. He had found her shaking like this once, frightened and injured, in her room. It had taken days for her to tell Robbie that their stepfather had shoved her down the stairs; the first of many violent acts that led to her death.

'Don't worry, little fella, I'll get you out of here.' Robbie was surprised by the conviction he felt.

Only then did he examine the cage's lock and saw that it might not be quite as easy as he thought.

★

Nikolas Rokoff's CD skipped again over the same three seconds of music. He stopped the disc the very moment he thought he heard a deep rumble. He froze, closing his eyes, and listening intently.

Years of hunting in the bush had finely honed each of his senses. He prided himself on being able to isolate the different scents in a herd, picking out a zebra's trail amid a hundred migrating wildebeests. He tuned out the generator noise and heard a deep metallic resonance. It lasted only for a second, but he had no doubt that it wasn't part of the ship's normal operations.

He picked his small Smith & Wesson 317 pistol from the table and secreted it in the folds of his suit jacket. It was small and lightweight enough to go unnoticed. Then he walked out on to the deck.

Rokoff immediately stepped into a pool of shadow, out of the range of the deck lights. He paused to listen, closing his eyes so they adjusted more quickly to the dark. With his eyes closed his other senses were heightened – and he immediately felt it. The boat was moving.

He opened his eyes and peered into the jungle. The clouds that had been obscuring the moon slid away to allow enough light for him to see that the boat was not only moving at quite a pace in the darkness but it had slewed sideways.

Rokoff noticed the anchor chain was coiled on deck. It normally took a diesel motor to lift the heavy chain, but somehow this had been carried out in utter silence. An act of sabotage that meant that the boat was now dangerously out of control. He knew he should alert the captain, but Rokoff hadn't survived as a hunter by panicking. His eyes scanned the boat for any sign of the intruder; any irregular shape against the sharp angular lines of the vessel.

Then he noticed wet footprints heading through a hatch, into the hull of the boat. Rokoff slipped one hand into his jacket, his fingers wrapping around the sculpted hilt of his pistol and carefully he followed the prints inside.

14

Tarzan clung to the narrow ladder rungs bolted on the side of the freighter's smokestack. The deck perimeter was illuminated, but the main structure in the middle was dark and lifeless. He had raised the anchor chain intending to cause chaos, but was disappointed that none of the crew had spilled on to the deck in panic.

He bristled when he saw Rokoff emerge from his cabin. His instinct to attack was strong, but Tarzan was no fool. He needed the Russian to lead him into the belly of the steel beast so he could find Karnath. He watched intently as the hunter disappeared through another door.

Tarzan jumped lightly on to the cabin roof; before he dropped to the deck he caught a sound in the distance. The river's voice was changing into a roar. Time was against him, but he still paused. Tracking quarry should never be rushed. Then, Tarzan silently leaped to the deck and followed Rokoff inside.

The stench in the claustrophobic corridor hit Tarzan hard. Civilisation: sweat, engine fumes, sickening food aromas and stale cigarette smoke. It all churned his stomach.

He zeroed in on the gentle creak of a closing hatchway ahead. He had ventured into underground cave systems before, but there was something about the man-made corridors that made him feel trapped. He stopped at the top of steel steps descending to another dark deck below and sniffed the air. Something was not right. He placed one foot on the hard steel step – then heard the noise behind him and whirled round in a low crouch, ready to fight.

Rokoff stood in the middle of the corridor. The open door next to him revealed where he had been hiding. He held Robbie around the throat with one arm, his other hand pressed a gun to the boy's head. Robbie was pale, although he didn't look frightened. If anything, Tarzan thought he looked angry. The Russian smiled as he studied Tarzan.

'So, we meet at last,' said Rokoff in a low voice. 'Look at you. A legend . . . and here you are.'

Tarzan judged the distance to Rokoff – it was too great. The Russian could easily kill Robbie and turn the gun on him.

'Can you speak, ape-man?' taunted Rokoff. 'Have you come for your little friend below? I assumed a mighty predator like you would have made more challenging prey. I expected more. You are a disappointment.'

Rokoff's words dripped with sarcasm, intended to push Tarzan into a reckless attack. But the words had no effect on him and failed to invoke any emotion other than the one Tarzan was already feeling towards Rokoff – pure hatred.

'Where Karnath?' Rokoff didn't see Robbie's gaze flicker towards the causeway leading to the deck below, but Tarzan did.

'So you give them names, do you? Like pets?' Rokoff taunted. Again, Tarzan didn't rise to the bait. The Russian renewed his grip on the pistol and pushed it hard against Robbie's temple. 'I want to know if you are human or an animal. Are you going to save your friend here before I blow his feeble brains out all over this boat? Or will you save your little ape down below? Either way you will be responsible for . . .'

Rokoff trailed off in amazement. Tarzan quickly headed down the steps towards Karnath. Even Robbie gave a startled gasp at Tarzan's choice to abandon them.

At that moment, Paulvitch and two crewmen

came slouching around the corner to see Tarzan quickly vanishing below deck, and Rokoff holding a prisoner.

'What's going on?' Paulvitch spluttered.

Then the lights went out.

In the pitch black there was a sudden rush of movement and Rokoff felt something heavy slam across the back of his head. He involuntarily pulled the trigger and the muzzle flash briefly illuminated a crewman's startled face. He felt a crushing weight against his stomach and Robbie slipped from his grasp.

'The lights!' Rokoff screamed.

He groped blindly along the corridor, navigating towards the deck by instinct alone. He needed to get outside before Tarzan discovered what he had done with Karnath.

Then he heard an inhuman bellow reverberate through the ship.

★

Tarzan stared at Karnath's empty cage. Jane and Robbie crouched in front of it examining traces of black hair that had fallen where Karnath had struggled. Tarzan could smell the ape's scent and his fingers touched flecks of blood in the cage. He roared again.

'Rokoff's men must've taken him the moment they found me,' said Robbie, massaging his temple. 'I managed to get away. Made it up one level before bumping into Rokoff. Karnath can't be far.' He was still in shock from their ambush. The moment Tarzan turned his back on rescuing him, Jane had turned the lights off from where she'd been hiding and hammered Rokoff across the head with a fire extinguisher. Then she pushed him down the steps a second before the gunshot went off. Robbie was pretty sure Rokoff had killed one of his own men in the confusion.

Tarzan raced for the door as Robbie spoke. Before he could reach it, it suddenly clanged shut and the locking wheel spun closed. Tarzan strained to open it. His muscles tensed until Robbie thought they would pop from under his skin, but the door held fast.

Jane looked around, realising that was their only exit. 'They've locked us in!'

'Great,' snarled Robbie. 'Did you actually have a plan for this rescue?'

Tarzan ignored them and examined the hold doors several metres above them. The hold's walls were smooth and featureless. Desperate, Tarzan ran for the corner, trying to bounce from one wall to the next to gain height, but it was no use. Time and time again he dropped back to the floor.

There were voices overhead and footsteps running across the deck. Even though the conversations were muffled, panic was unmistakable. Then the boat shuddered with a high-pitched squeal of tearing metal. The entire vessel slammed to a halt with such force they were all thrown across the hold – along with an array of Rokoff's hunting equipment. They hit the wall as the vessel shook furiously once more.

The boat rose and fell as if a giant hand had plucked it free from the water then hurled it back down with terrible force. Jane found herself sliding up the wall as the room rotated around them – the boat was listing. A jagged rock suddenly punctured through the steel close to her head. She screamed as water poured through.

Tarzan stabilised himself on all fours then scrambled towards Jane – but had to leap aside as another rock slammed through the hull just centimetres from his head.

Robbie lost his footing and slipped along a wall, which was now the sloping floor. The boat stopped rolling and remained tilted at an extreme angle. Another rock sliced effortlessly through the metal hull and passed between Robbie's legs narrowly missing him.

Torrents of murky brown water poured into the boat, rapidly filling the room. Robbie groped for the hatch, but the angle of the room put it beyond his reach.

'Help!' Jane yelled.

Robbie joined in. 'Let us out of here!' Water was already up to their waists.

Tarzan studied the situation with the calmness of one who had looked death in the face so many times that he felt no fear.

The sloping room had positioned him slightly closer to the edge of the hold doors. With a powerful jump, Tarzan rebounded from the wall and sailed high into the doors. They buckled from the impact and it looked like he was about to fall onto the jagged rocks and twisted metal below. But he some-how edged his fingers in the gap between the doors. Now hanging, he pulled himself up with his power-ful arms and braced his legs against the other door intent on pushing it open.

Robbie and Jane could only watch helplessly while treading water. The hold's chains held firm – but still Tarzan pushed. The corner of the metal door began to creak out of shape. Pushing from the inside with all his strength, Tarzan managed to peel the steel apart just wide enough for him to clamber through.

Robbie could only hope he wouldn't forget about the two of them, trapped in the hold.

★

Having squeezed through the hatchway, Tarzan braced himself on the sharply sloping deck and assessed the situation. The strong current had flung the ship on to jagged rocks near the bank. The sheer weight of water had forced the ship to keel to port, white water frothing around it.

The lights on the deck flashed as the generator room was filled with water. As Tarzan watched, crewmen slid off the boat and into the dark river. The lucky ones struck the rocks below and were killed instantly. The unlucky ones splashed into the deeper water, which became a writhing mass of limbs as dozens of crocodiles, their dull eyes glinting in the ship's lights, closed in for the feast. Those who landed in shallower water faced a different threat. Huge silver bodies glided under the water's surface, homing in on men swimming to shore – carnivorous Goliath tiger fish, their teeth-filled jaws severing entire limbs with a single bite.

Most people would have been repulsed by the violence in front of them, but not Tarzan. For him it was a simple matter of hunter and prey; the circle of life. The ship lurched again, the deck flattening out. He spotted Rokoff near the prow. A huddle of men surrounded him carrying an unconscious form: Karnath.

With a bellow, Tarzan charged forwards, hampered by the inclined deck. Rokoff glanced around in alarm and hurried his men towards the end of the boat. Tarzan would not let them leave with the young ape.

In ten quick bounds, Tarzan crossed the ship. Two huge crewmen, double the size of silverbacks, blocked his path. Tarzan charged into one – slamming him against the steel wall. The man slumped in agony as the second thug grabbed Tarzan around the shoulders, locking his hands behind his neck. But Tarzan just flexed his powerful shoulder muscles and the thug cried out in pain as both his arms were dislocated under the immense pressure.

Tarzan spun around, fury burning in his eyes as he grabbed the man around the throat.

'Please . . . don't kill me!' croaked the brute fearfully, his arms hanging limp at his sides.

'Tarzan not kill,' he said, and the crewman breathed a sigh of relief. 'But *Pisah* must eat.'

With that Tarzan hurled the man over the ship's rail into a shoal of circling tiger fish. For a second their green-silver scales flashed in the ship's lights, then the water turned blood red.

Before Tarzan could turn to Rokoff, the boat's lights died as the generator gave a final rattle, plunging the boat into chaotic shadows. Tarzan could sense where his target was. He could hear his every move . . . but he could also hear Jane and Robbie's yells of panic from inside the hold. He hesitated, for once unsure what to do.

Just then thunder rumbled. It sounded unusual, a constant stream of noise that didn't die out. Before Tarzan could react, a spear of light stabbed down from the sky, blinding him. He sank to his knees, shielding his eyes.

The thunder boomed louder and the wind became a hurricane that pushed him off balance. Tarzan slid across the deck – the railing preventing him from falling amongst the predators feasting below.

The intense light burned his eyes. Squinting, he could just make out a large black shape descending from the sky. Tarzan was not afraid of anything, but this experience confused him. He could just hear Rokoff's voice above the continuous thunder, ordering people towards the monster.

Still shielding his eyes, Tarzan saw Karnath being loaded into the machine, Rokoff following him – shouting at another figure who quickly approached Tarzan.

'Alexis! No!'

Tarzan could see nothing more than Paulvitch's silhouette, but he could smell the man's distinctive vile odour.

'So you're Rokoff's legendary white ape?' sneered Paulvitch. 'Not so mighty now.'

He prodded Tarzan's arm with a Taser stun gun. A violent electrical charge surged through Tarzan and it felt as if every nerve in his body was on fire. With a spasm he collapsed on to the deck.

'Alexis! We are leaving!' Rokoff shouted.

Paulvitch ignored Rokoff. He was a little man, never passing up an opportunity to pick on a weak target. His tone was triumphant. 'That's what your little ape friend felt. Enough voltage to stop a charging lion. Hurts, doesn't it?'

Paulvitch lunged again. To his amazement, Tarzan grabbed his hand, crushing the man's fingers around the Taser so hard that both his bone and the plastic casing cracked. He kicked Paulvitch in the stomach and sent the tiny man sailing through the air, slamming into the bulkhead.

Tarzan clambered to his feet, weakened from the electric shock and beaten back by the downdraught from the machine. He saw the whimpering Paulvitch climb next to Rokoff. Tarzan quickened his pace – but was stopped as gunfire raked the deck, kicking up sparks and forcing him to back down.

As the machine lifted into the air, the powerful spotlight swung away, no longer blinding Tarzan. Rokoff sat in the doorway aiming a hunting rifle at him. Tarzan was an open target, an easy shot.

But no bullet came.

Rokoff lowered the weapon as the aircraft banked over the jungle beyond Tarzan's reach. He yelled in frustration, his voice booming over the fading thunder.

The boat suddenly lurched underfoot as it rolled off the rocks towards deeper water.

Jane's voice cut through the darkness. 'Tarzan! Help!'

Tarzan raced back towards the hold to save his friends. His mind was reeling. Why hadn't Rokoff killed him? He couldn't be sure, but he swore he caught the trace of a smile on the Russian's face before he disappeared into the darkness. But the hunt was over. Tarzan knew there was no way he could track an airborne opponent.

Karnath was lost.

15

Clark had never visited Sango so frequently. The loggers usually stocked up with supplies just once a month, only making the long trek into town if it was absolutely necessary. That had been his own rule to maintain absolute secrecy over their operation. He didn't want the locals getting used to seeing them in town and he had no intention of getting arrested. He had spent time in jails around the world before, all because he hadn't been careful enough. However, Tarzan was making him break his own rules.

At the same time he could sense Archie becoming ever more anxious since their encounters with Rokoff. Clark admitted that it had been a mistake to take the Russian's claims of being a conservationist at face value. But although Rokoff had turned out to be a liar, Clark felt pleased his plan to prove Tarzan's identity remained on track, with Robbie still travelling with the ape-man, recording evidence on his camcorder.

After his tussle in the jungle when out looking for Jane, when the pain in his leg grew unbearable, Mister David agreed to drive Clark to revisit the medical team in Sango. Worryingly, when the doctor took a look at his leg she declared that the leopard wound was worse than they first thought. The antibiotics were keeping infection at bay and it would heal, but Clark would probably have a limp for the rest of his life.

He knew it could have been worse. He could have lost the leg: he could have been killed. And, for the first time in his life, Clark realised that he was a middle-aged man running around a jungle looking to get rich. He had been doing that all his life, but wondered if his time would soon be up.

Two cold Tusker beers helped him silence his doubts and he gave a fistful of francs to the Internet café owner to help him log into his email. Clark was not computer literate and, without Robbie around, his technical skills were limited. He made sure the café owner couldn't see the messages that were waiting for him in his inbox. Amongst them was one from 'William'. The name was unfamiliar but the subject line 'Tarzan' immediately got his attention.

Clark read through the message twice to make sure he fully understood it. His hopes were lifted.

Dear Clark,

Allow me to introduce myself: I am William Cecil Clayton, or, as my more formal title now reads, Lord Greystoke. I recently inherited this title when my father sadly passed away two weeks ago. I must say your email intrigued me. My father was forever receiving messages from people claiming that Lord and Lady Greystoke, had survived the plane crash with their unborn child, but of course they were nothing more than confidence tricksters and scam artists. This business all started when a French UN officer, called Paul D'Arnot, claimed he had found a boy living in the jungle who was my father's nephew. Needless to say, his story proved false, but it didn't stop others from trying.

My father grew wary and demanded hard evidence that his nephew, my cousin, could possibly still be alive and he took your messages as nothing more than another extortionist trying to squeeze money from us.

I should warn you that I have now taken my seat in the House of Lords and have powerful influence, even in the Congo. However, should your claims prove to have merit, then there is a substantial reward for whoever finds my cousin alive. After all, that would mean *he* is the current holder of the title and owner of the Greystoke estate.

Should you uncover any compelling evidence of my cousin's existence then contact me directly. Do not contact the media: that will void any reward. And, should you think of trying to fake any claims, then rest assured I will find you.

Yours sincerely,

Lord Greystoke

That was all Clark needed to convince himself that he wasn't wasting his life in the jungle. He logged off the computer and limped out of the café on his crutch. The owner, a young Congolese man in his twenties, was sitting in the open window frame watching him carefully. Clark knew he went by the name of Kwasi.

'You always here with the younger man, *non*?' Kwasi asked in French-accented English.

Clark stopped in the doorway, annoyed that he had been recognised. If he was going to be handing out wads of francs then he was going to start getting noticed and now his crutch made him all the more memorable.

'Why d'you ask?'

Kwasi smiled, flashing his perfect white teeth. He was used to never receiving straight answers. He wagged a finger at Clark. 'Yes, you are. You cannot fool me.'

'Well, I tried,' said Clark forcing a smile and turning to leave. He didn't have time to chat with a grinning fool. He stepped on to the porch when Kwasi spoke up again.

'I just thought you would be interested . . . never mind.'

Clark turned and cocked his head. 'Interested in what?'

Kwasi's eyes darted to the pocket Clark had stuffed his cash in. The boy was observant, he'd give him that. It was also clearly the end of the conversation unless more money was offered. Clark reluctantly rolled out a note. Kwasi took it and stared at it critically.

'That's all you're gettin', mate,' said Clark. 'I don't pay when I don't know what I'm gettin'. Let me decide if it's worth more.'

Clark reached to take the note away but Kwasi's

hand moved fast, stashing the money in his ripped jeans. He flashed another toothy smile.

'I like you,' said Kwasi. 'You give me good custom. Which is why, when I hear there is a man in the town downriver, asking questions about an American teenager . . . then I should maybe worry about keeping my business flowing, *non?*'

Although the nearest town was almost fifty miles away, news and gossip travelled fast between fishermen and black-market traders. New faces were always top of the list, just in case they posed a threat to the town's illegal lifeblood.

'Is he comin' this way?' Clark asked. Kwasi nodded. 'You know what he's been askin' about?'

'Just about him. Not you. The man is an American also.'

Clark had asked Robbie nothing about his past, but this development was making him wonder about Jane's comment concerning Robbie's stepfather. Would the anonymity policy he set among the camp workers come back to bite him? He pushed a bundle of notes into Kwasi's hand. It was probably more than the café owner made in a month.

'Keep your ears open. If he comes here, tell him nothin' and see no one else does, OK?' Kwasi nodded enthusiastically. 'Try an' find out more about him. Let me know.'

Clark headed to the jeep to wait for Mister David. This was worrying news. He only hoped that whatever Robbie had done, it wasn't going to have repercussions on the camp. Clark sat in the jeep and pulled out his sat phone. He stared at it wondering if he should let Robbie know, or wait until they had proof of Tarzan's link to Greystoke.

★

Being rescued from the freighter's hold was a relatively simple, if frightening, affair. The water inside had continued to rise, forcing Robbie and Jane up towards the hatch. Jane was able to use her backpack as a flotation device and they both clung to it. While it was terrifying to be sloshed around in utter darkness, they were unharmed. Tarzan only had to lean down into the hatch and pull them out. They ran to the stern as the big ship wallowed into deeper water and Tarzan pushed them to jump into the branches of an overhanging tree before they were pulled further away from the shoreline.

Jane secured her backpack and made the jump with ease. Robbie hesitated – unlike Jane, he had never experienced a giddying free-running ride through the jungle canopy with Tarzan. In the half-moonlight, Robbie saw the gap between the boat and tree increasing. With a deep breath he took a running jump, closing his eyes as he did so. He struck a thick branch, which swayed wildly and almost threw him off. Jane pulled him up to safety and Tarzan joined them moments later.

Exhausted, they watched the stricken vessel slowly vanish beneath the river's surface. The crocodiles and tiger fish, bloated from their feast, disappeared into the night. Tarzan declared they would sleep in the tree, for safety, then said nothing further. Looking morose, he just gazed in the direction Rokoff had fled.

'Maybe we should go back and check the rest of your family are OK?' said Jane after a weighty silence. 'They need you too.'

Tarzan nodded slowly. In the pale light, Robbie saw the pain on Tarzan's face. He felt wretched, knowing he was to blame for bringing Rokoff into their lives.

'We're not going back,' Robbie stated firmly.

'There's no way we can chase Rokoff in a helicopter,' Jane stated flatly.

'You're wrong,' he said. 'We *can* find him.' He could hardly believe he was suggesting this when Jane had just given him an opportunity to see Tarzan's home.

Fatigue had worn Jane's patience down. 'How?'

'With this.' Robbie held up the GPS that he dug

out of Jane's backpack. A blip flashed on the screen. 'Now we know exactly where he is.'

Jane's face lit up in a smile. 'How is that possible?'

'When Rokoff pushed the gun against my head I slipped a GPS tracker in his jacket. After being treated like that, I really didn't want to see him get away scot-free.'

He was surprised when Jane promptly hugged him, laughing gleefully. She snatched the GPS from Robbie and showed it to Tarzan.

'This is where Karnath is! We can still find him! By the look of things they've already stopped.'

Tarzan looked at the flashing GPS in confusion. He clearly didn't understand. Robbie smiled and leaned back, closing his eyes; it would be amusing to hear Jane explain the tracking device to the wild man. He fell asleep moments later.

★

Jane woke from a deep slumber, instantly aware that a small gecko was scampering across her jeans. The little lizard was no threat, so she gently shook her leg to frighten it enough to run away. Not so long ago she would have freaked out over such an encounter and it made her realise just how much she was feeling at home in the wild.

She heard Robbie speaking in a low voice down

on the ground. There was no sign of Tarzan, but Robbie was eating fruit as he talked into his sat phone.

Jane clambered down the broad tree trunk. The tree grew at a slight angle, and its trunk was pitted with knots and handholds that made it ideal for climbing. Robbie hung up the phone before she jumped the last metre to the ground.

'Was that my dad?'

'Clark,' said Robbie.

'Worrying about us again? Where's Tarzan?'

'He said he'd scout the path ahead.' He pointed to several unusual fruits stacked on a stone. 'He left breakfast.'

Jane sniffed them. She couldn't identify the smell so pulled one open, revealing green pulp inside. She took a small bite and it tasted good. She ate three before noticing that Robbie was looking thoughtfully across the river.

'What's on your mind?'

Robbie didn't respond. It was as if he hadn't even heard her. When she gently touched his shoulder he flinched.

'What's wrong?' she asked, now more concerned.

Robbie didn't answer at first. He handed her the water canteen he was holding and Jane took a long gulp to wash down the fruit.

'My sister . . .' Robbie was finding it difficult to get the words out. He took a deep breath and tried again. 'I did a little more digging into Sophie's death.'

'Yeah, you said. You didn't kill your stepfather, so don't worry about it, and what happened to your sister—'

Robbie cut her off. 'That's the point! I didn't kill him and I wish I had!'

'No, you don't.'

'You don't know what I think,' said Robbie in a whisper. He stared at the ground to collect his thoughts, then looked at her as if gauging her reaction. 'I wish he was dead. And you know why? Because he's a liar. He told the cops that not only did I try to kill him . . . but I killed Sophie too!'

Jane was horrified. 'Are you sure?'

Robbie was choking with emotion, glad to finally get it all off his chest. 'Positive. I'm now wanted for killing my own sister and the man who really did it is testifying against me and offering a cash reward! There's a worldwide manhunt out to find me!'

16

The tracker beacon always lay just ahead; always out of reach. Robbie had checked the GPS screen almost every half hour when they first started their hike through the jungle, but as the day wore on monitored their progress less and less.

Tarzan pushed them on, desperate to take to the trees and speed ahead but forced to slow down and wait for his guides. Robbie could see the frustration in his face and guessed that Tarzan disliked having to rely on others to lead the way. It went against every instinct the ape-man had.

Robbie welcomed the fast pace even if it was exhausting. He had taken the backpack from Jane, his clothes were drenched with sweat and he could barely feel his legs, but it kept his mind focused on the task at hand. He felt relieved that he had finally told Jane his problem. Somebody was looking for him, but he still didn't know who. Was it his step-father? The cops? A private investigator?

Jane walked beside him saying very little. Robbie caught her occasionally glancing thoughtfully at him. He was starting to get paranoid – did she doubt his story about Sophie's death? Did she think he really *was* responsible?

As his mind whirred with doubt and guilt, the day was measured only in unfaltering footsteps. Minutes blurred into hours and muscles began to throb until Robbie was thankful for nightfall.

Dark clouds rolled in and fat raindrops stung as they fell. Tarzan found shelter under a fallen tree, snapping off branches to fashion a nest as the apes had taught him during his childhood. Robbie thought it was a waste of time until he lay down and discovered the branches had been woven together to form a comfortable bed that supported his aching limbs. He quickly fell asleep, lulled by the sound of the rain, but was haunted by bad dreams during the night.

The next morning Tarzan woke them in pre-dawn light, eager to move on.

Jane noticed that the GPS tracker had remained stationary overnight too. Robbie worried that Rokoff had found the tracker and thrown it away, but he didn't dare share his fears with the other two. Jane continued to be silent and withdrawn and it looked as if the pace of their hunt was beginning to wear her down as well.

Tarzan, too, spoke little, pushing them on with grim determination, pausing to read the signs in the earth and pick out the most direct animal trails. Robbie suspected that every time he vanished ahead, it was to clear their path from potential dangers that would slow them down. Once he returned covered in flecks of blood. Whether it was from a battle or a meal that hadn't escaped him, Robbie didn't know. They pressed on through the rain and didn't stop as lightning flickered through low clouds and thunder boomed with such fury that the jungle came alive with the shrieks of birds and monkeys.

Without the sun as a guide it was impossible to judge how much time had passed. Only by glancing at the clock on his sat phone did Robbie realise that hours were racing by. He almost didn't notice the jungle becoming less dense and the sickly humidity decrease. He nearly bumped into Jane before he looked up and realised they were standing on a lush green hill with knots of trees thinning out as the ground sloped away. In the distance, through the veil of rain, the grass gave way to rows of cultivated fields. Robbie felt a renewed hope at the signs of civilisation. He checked the GPS and noticed the marker was moving again.

Tarzan wanted to follow the moving blip directly. However, Robbie convinced him they would be better heading to the location where Rokoff had spent a day. For all they knew the Russian had left Karnath where he'd stopped and was moving on.

So they pressed towards the fields. The storm passed and the moonlight guided their progress. Robbie guessed it must be close to midnight and that they had been walking in the darkness without a break. Just as he was thinking of insisting they stop, he saw white lights ahead, the beginnings of a sprawling town much larger than Sango.

'Where are we?' asked Jane.

Robbie glanced at the GPS. It was a straightforward interface that revealed no detail other than the distance and direction of Rokoff's blip to the east, heading towards the border.

'Can't be sure but at least we're still in the Democratic Republic of Congo. We've been heading steadily south-east. Rokoff's in that direction, still a day ahead but according to the waypoint marker, he spent almost twenty-four hours here.'

Tarzan studied the lights suspiciously. 'If Rokoff not here then we go.'

Jane shook her head. 'No, we decided, we need to find out why he spent so much time here. Maybe he left Karnath? We need to look around. Ask questions.'

For the first time, Robbie could see apprehension on Tarzan's face. Being so close to civilisation made him nervous.

'I don't know about you guys, but the idea of walking around a possibly dangerous town at night isn't that appealing. I vote we sleep here. Check it out in the daytime,' he said.

To Robbie's surprise, Tarzan nodded. 'Yes. Town not safe.'

They found a nearby tree and settled in the low branches. The air was far less humid than in the jungle, and Robbie enjoyed the cool breeze. The sounds around him were different here; insects and frogs chirped in the darkness but there were no cries of monkeys or birds.

They entered the town early next morning. Circled by ploughed fields, it was a simple place with ramshackle buildings made from mud bricks and sheets of corrugated iron that had been daubed with bright colours. No structure stood higher than a single storey, except an old weather-beaten church. Electricity came only from noisy petrol generators at the back of bigger properties.

Robbie led the way, Tarzan keeping uncharacteristically behind. He was clearly ill at ease, his eyes darting from the single-storey huts to the rubbish-strewn alleys between them. Market vendors were already beginning to set up their wares before the sun grew too hot. Carts were filled with peanuts still on their root branches, long brown cassavas and a variety of spices. Tarzan tensed when they passed a stall with several dead crocodiles hanging from hooks, a buck of some kind and several monkeys that had been dried in the sun and shrivelled beyond recognition.

'A place of murder,' he muttered.

'It's food,' said Jane in a low voice, gently pushing Tarzan onwards as he glared at the old man behind the cart. 'We don't eat it raw, remember. We cook it.'

'You burn good flesh.'

Robbie was relieved that Jane didn't pursue the argument. He had been afraid that Tarzan would stand out with his bare barrel chest and ragged cargo shorts, but he almost fitted in with the, admittedly less muscular, townsfolk. It was Jane who drew the most attention as a blonde in a place where dark hair was the norm.

Ignoring Tarzan's grumbling, Robbie led them into the heart of the town. A pair of stray dogs started barking at Tarzan, baring their teeth as they challenged the newcomers. Tarzan dropped to all fours, bringing himself almost nose to nose with the dogs and flashed his own teeth, issuing a long deep growl. The strays yelped, tails folded between their legs.

Robbie looked from the bizarre scene to an old man who sat on his porch with a toothless smile creasing his face. He took Tarzan's arm, his muscles feeling like iron, and tried to pull him upright. Tarzan didn't budge.

'That's enough of that,' said Robbie from the corner of his mouth, his eyes fixed on the old man. 'You're making us look weird.'

Tarzan stood, wondering why Jane was hiding her smile. Robbie approached the old man.

'*Bonjour, parlez-vous anglais?*' Robbie only knew a few French phrases and he hoped his accent wasn't too hard to understand.

The man nodded, still smiling. 'Yes, yes. Your friend thinks he's a dog!' That sent the man off into a fit of laughter.

Robbie humoured the old man. 'No, he thinks he's a monkey.' That appeared to please him. 'We're looking for some friends of ours who passed through here. They look like us. They flew here.'

'Ah! They think they are birds!' The man howled with laughter.

Robbie looked at Jane for help but she shrugged. 'They flew in a helicopter.' He indicated with his hands but was afraid the man was too simple to understand.

The man wiped tears from his eyes and pointed across town. 'Of course they did! They came, I saw it. The airfield is over there.' He pointed across town, still chuckling to himself.

Robbie's pulse quickened. They were on the right track. 'Did they fly away from here?'

The man shook his head. 'No. They are not birds.' He stared at Robbie deadpan. Robbie expected the man to break into foolish laughter again, but evidently the comedy was over and the man's smile faded as he regarded Robbie as if he was the idiot. 'They had engine trouble,' the man clarified. 'I could hear it from my bed.'

'Are they still here?' asked Robbie excitedly.

The man shrugged and gazed down the street without speaking. Obviously his entertainment was over. Robbie thanked him and they threaded their way through the town in the direction indicated. The streets were getting busier and several battered cars and pick-up trucks passed by playing loud African music and stinking of petrol fumes. Tarzan was alarmed, and Robbie became aware of the many hostile looks they were receiving. Even though Sango was a rogue trading post on the banks of the river, it felt friendlier than this shanty town. He was thankful they had Tarzan with them as their own personal security.

On the edge of town they found the airfield, although that was a glamorous name for a strip of dirt in the grass. A small shelter with a bench and corrugated iron roof resembled a bus stop rather than an airport departure lounge. Behind it was a large metal shed that acted as a hangar. The rusting iron panels on the roof and walls were coming free. Several ancient vehicles were parked up around a large helicopter. The aircraft looked as old as the cars, rust covering the fuselage, but Tarzan recognised the machine that Rokoff had escaped in. An engine access hood was open just beneath the long drooping rotors. Two men perching on ladders worked on the complex engine within. Another two stood below, passing up tools. The hangar smelled of oil and aviation fuel, coming from the barrels stacked against one of the walls.

'Tarzan will fight!'

'Let me deal with this,' hissed Robbie. 'We're in civilisation now. We have rules to follow.' He approached the men, smiling and raising his hand in greeting. 'Hey, guys!'

The men stopped working and turned with hostile glances. The two at the foot of the ladders slowly walked towards Robbie. One, with a goatee beard, methodically wiped his hands on an oily rag, while the other folded his brawny arms.

'Nice helicopter,' said Robbie amiably. 'Got a little engine trouble?' The men glanced past Robbie as if he was insignificant, then lingered on Jane before finally staring at Tarzan, judging him to be the real threat. Robbie drew their attention back to himself, keeping his tone as friendly as possible. 'Some friends of ours rented it out. We wondered which way they went.'

'Friends?' growled the nearest thug.

Robbie glanced at Tarzan, sensing he was ready to attack. Robbie gave a small shake of his head. He had everything under control.

'The two Russians,' he said with a grin.

On hearing this, the two mechanics slid down the ladder and circled around Robbie, regarding him with undisguised hostility. One had an ugly scar splitting his nose and Robbie tried not to look at him too hard.

'Rokoff and Paulvitch,' said Robbie, determined not to be intimidated. 'We were supposed to meet them here but they went ahead.'

The split-nosed man started to laugh. It sounded more like a humourless dry cough. 'Rokoff is a friend of yours? But he didn't tell you where he was going?'

They obviously didn't believe him, but it was too late for Robbie to save face and change his story. 'Yep,' he said with a shrug. 'You know how he is.'

'Oh, we know,' said Split-nose. The smile dropped from his face and Robbie was surprised to see a wheel wrench had appeared in his hand. It had been hidden out of sight, hooked to the back of his belt. 'And you are no friends of his.'

He swung the wrench with lightning speed and a blinding pain struck Robbie's ribs. The air expelled from his lungs and he dropped to the floor. Split-nose's boot swung towards Robbie's face – but it never made contact.

Tarzan leaped over Robbie with a murderous howl. He cannoned into the mechanic with such ferocity that both men hit the floor and slid towards the chopper. The wrench arced towards Tarzan's head but Tarzan caught it. Bone crunched as Tarzan squeezed the man's wrist, then gave a sharp twist to the right. Split-nose screamed and his forearm bent at an unnatural angle. He dropped the wrench as two other mechanics jumped on to Tarzan's back before he could react.

Robbie fought for breath, unable to help. The hangar spun from the pain in his side. He heard Jane cry out, and turned to see the goateed man grab her hair, pulling it back.

'Get off her!' Robbie had tried to shout, but it came as nothing more than a wheeze. He ran to help, stumbling like a drunk. Robbie's fists targeted the man's kidneys. Goatee-man grunted in pain – before spinning around and punching Robbie squarely in the face. For a second, lights flashed behind Robbie's eyes and he crashed to the ground. He tasted blood and his nose felt swollen. Groggily he saw Jane run towards a workbench. Her injured assailant went after her.

Tarzan's attackers, meanwhile, slammed him into the chopper's fuselage and both men used their weight to pin him there. Tarzan had trouble maintaining a grip on their oily skin and they slipped from his grasp to deliver rapid blows to his stomach. The savage assault forced Tarzan to his knees.

Tarzan dropped – not in defeat, but in a calculated attack move. He grabbed the mechanic's foot and pulled sharply so that the man fell on his back, knocking himself out as he cracked his head on the floor. Tarzan then rolled onto his back and kicked his second attacker so hard that he was sent flying in to the cockpit window, cracking the plastic canopy.

Robbie tried to stand but the room was still spinning. He saw the goateed thug reach Jane and shove her against the bench, one hand around her neck. Robbie didn't have time to be concerned for Jane's safety as her flailing hand found a small blowtorch. She cracked the pint-sized gas canister over Goatee's head. The man staggered back but recovered quickly and lunged for her once again.

She squeezed the torch's trigger and a jet of blue flame erupted across the man's chest. He howled in agony as his oily clothes caught fire. Jane backed away, stunned at what she'd done. The man tore at his burning overalls, but couldn't remove the one-piece suit. Murder was etched across his face as he swung for Jane, knocking the blowtorch aside. Jane cried out as the man's strong hands closed around her windpipe, choking her.

With a ferocious howl that echoed through the hangar, Tarzan ran to Jane's aid.

He grabbed the burning man from behind and held him high over his head. Then, without a single tremor in his arms, Tarzan hurled the mechanic into the barrels.

'No!' yelled Robbie, but his swollen nose dampened his warning.

Tarzan had no knowledge of chemicals. He had no concept of what would happen when the man's burning clothes ignited the aviation fuel in the barrels. Luckily Jane did; she grabbed Tarzan's hand and pulled him towards the exit.

'Run!'

Fighting his muzziness, Robbie sprinted after them. The burning goateed man bounced from the barrels, tipping two over. He hit the floor hard and had no time to scream when he saw the yellow liquid spill from the barrels and wash towards him.

Robbie ran for the exit. He reached the hangar door just as the first explosion hit. With a mighty boom an orange fireball shot straight up, blowing a section of roof away.

The shockwave sent Robbie reeling into the split-nosed mechanic who was also scrambling to escape outside. They both fell as a second explosion tore through the building. Multiple fuel barrels exploded, streaking across the hangar like missiles. Two smashed into the helicopter, which then detonated with such fury the ageing aircraft was ripped in two. Robbie coughed as smoke began to drift over him and through streaming eyes, he watched as the entire building groaned then collapsed on itself, black smoke and vivid orange flames mushrooming out.

Tarzan and Jane were sprawled on the ground a little further away.

'This civilisation?' he growled.

'No,' gasped Jane. 'We're just having a bad day!'

Tarzan strode over to Split-nose who was crawling away from Robbie. He picked the thug up by his collar and roughly shook him.

'Where Rokoff?'

Split-nose coughed and tried to pull himself free but he was too weak.

'He's gone. Took a truck and went yesterday.'

'Where Karnath?' Tarzan growled.

'What? I don't know who that is.'

Tarzan shook the man fiercely. 'Karnath!'

'I don't know!'

Easily holding the man in one hand, Tarzan walked over to the burning hangar. The heat was severe, even from several metres away so Tarzan held the man as close as he could to the flames. Split-nose shrieked as the heat singed his skin.

'Karnath!' yelled Tarzan.

Jane ran as close as she could bear. 'Tarzan! Wait!' She peered at the thug without a trace of remorse. 'He won't hesitate in throwing you into the fire. Now tell us about the gorilla Rokoff had with him. Why does he want it? Who is he?'

Split-nose was suddenly in a talkative mood as the flames crept nearer. 'He's a hunter. I've worked with him before. He's the best in the world. You want anything, he can get it. The ape is for a collector in Uganda. Ataro Okeke.'

Robbie crossed over to them and was alarmed by the rage on Tarzan's face.

'Where is he now?' said Robbie.

'He wanted to drive to Tanganyika. He couldn't wait for the chopper to be repaired and we couldn't have flown over the border anyway.'

'Where's he going to sell the ape?' Jane demanded.

The man was now crying from the pain singeing his back and legs. 'I don't know! He only said Uganda . . . I don't know!'

For a second, Robbie thought Jane was going to order Tarzan to hurl the man into the fire, but then he saw compassion cross her face.

'Tarzan won't kill you . . .'

'Thank you! Thank you!'

'I haven't finished. He won't kill you *if* you find us a jeep and all the equipment we need to follow Rokoff. Believe me, if we find out you're lying, Tarzan will be back. And no matter where you hide, he will find you.'

17

They drove steadily eastwards for a full day. The terrified mechanic had assured Jane that the jeep was the best in the town even if it lacked air conditioning and the cab was stifling; at least the suspension levelled out most of the potholes on the primitive road that led towards Tanganyika.

It had taken a great deal of persuasion to get Tarzan inside the jeep. He had never been in a moving vehicle before and every sound made his head turn in alarm. After a couple of hours he grew accustomed to the noises and began to relax.

Robbie drove. He was very glad they were no longer walking as his ribs hurt so much from the fight that he was sure a few were broken. He kept his eyes on the road, occasionally glancing at the GPS screen he'd hooked on to the dashboard. Rokoff had stopped for a couple of hours ahead, but now appeared to be moving again very slowly. The rocking vehicle sent Jane to sleep, while Tarzan gazed out of the window at the endless lines of cultivated fields. Civilisation had left a sour taste in his mouth.

After an hour of silence, and with Jane still fast asleep, Robbie spoke up.

'You don't like towns, do you?'

'Jungle safer.' That made Robbie laugh. Tarzan looked at him curiously. 'Why laugh?'

'Because since I've been in the jungle I've been chased by just about every animal, almost eaten alive by ants, trampled by hippos, swallowed by crocodiles . . . and you think it's safe?'

'They eat for food. They attack for food. Men attack for hatred and anger.'

'Not everybody is like that. Look at us. Look at D'Arnot.' Tarzan's brow furrowed at the mention of his old friend. 'There are lots of good people out there. What about your family? The Greystokes?'

'Tarzan family live in jungle.'

'Your foster family, maybe. You understand, foster parents? They're the ones who look after you even though they're not your real parents. I understand that family can be . . . complicated. I know my family is looking for me.' He had no intention of explaining his complex family life to Tarzan. 'Whether or not you admit that your real parents died in a plane crash, leaving you out in the jungle to fend for yourself –

that's your own decision. But if you do have a family out there . . . somewhere in civilisation, then don't you think you owe it to them to say you're alive? That you're safe?'

'Tarzan happy here,' he said simply.

Robbie didn't have a response to that. He couldn't recall the last time he had been happy. Not for the first time he was having doubts about whether Clark's plan to hand Tarzan over to the Greystokes and claim the reward money was the right thing to do.

Robbie reached up to the sun visor where the video camera was wedged and stopped it recording. Tucked in his pocket, the palm-sized camcorder had endured everything the jungle had thrown at them. He had been taking fragments of video ever since they embarked on their rescue mission and hoped some of it would help convince the Greystokes, but he still needed footage of Lord Greystoke's private aircraft in the jungle.

He slipped the camera into his pocket then turned his attention back to the road and suddenly slammed on the brakes. The truck skidded in the dirt, jolting Jane awake.

'What is it?' said Jane, instantly alert.

She followed Robbie's and Tarzan's gaze outside. They had crested a hill, revealing the landscape beyond. Instead of ploughed fields or jungle, the horizon was a deep blue. A colossal stretch of water lay in front of them.

'Is that the sea?' asked Jane, confused.

'Lake Tanganyika,' murmured Robbie. He glanced at the GPS. 'Tanzania's on the other shore, then north into Uganda. That's where Rokoff's heading. Problem is, we can't go. We don't have our passports. I didn't think we'd be running across Africa.'

Jane sighed in disappointment. 'We've got to do something!'

'Passports?' repeated Tarzan.

'Pieces of paper that allow us to cross the border into another country.' Robbie looked to Jane for help.

'Borders are . . . are the edge of another territory. Like between you and the *targarni*,' She said. Tarzan nodded in understanding.

'And without passports, we can't cross,' said Robbie.

Tarzan was unruffled. 'No border stops Tarzan!'

★

Crossing the second largest lake in the world proved to be easier than any of them had anticipated. The great lake ran for nearly seven hundred kilometres north to south, but was not very wide from east to west. In tracking Rokoff they had reached the northern shore and only had to cross the fifty kilometres to enter Tanzania on the opposite side. After that it was a relatively short hop into Uganda. They didn't have any money to catch the regular ferries from the northern DRC city of Uvira, but Robbie used his experience in such matters to smuggle themselves aboard a smaller cargo boat that was bound for Kigoma in Tanzania. Tarzan had been reluctant to venture on board the ship, but was persuaded when Jane pointed out that it was the only way they could catch up with Rokoff who, like them, had been slowed by the great lake.

The journey lasted almost four hours and they took the opportunity to rest. Robbie fell into a fitful sleep and even Tarzan curled up in their hiding place in the hold and slept.

They arrived in Kigoma at nightfall, which helped the three of them to slip off the boat and through the docks unnoticed. Tarzan was keen to leave the town as quickly as possible. According to the GPS, Rokoff was rapidly heading north-east towards Uganda. From the speed of his progress, it was clear that he had taken another vehicle and Robbie warned Tarzan that there was no way they could catch up on foot. Tarzan suggested that they should take another car. Jane tried to explain the concept of theft to him, but Tarzan still had no real understanding that people could *own* things. Robbie ended their moral debate by reassuring Jane they would return the vehicle afterwards so technically they would only be borrowing it.

Robbie liberated a sturdy four-by-four and they put as much distance as they could between them and civilisation. Robbie drove through the night along a dirt and gravel track until he couldn't keep his eyes open any longer. They parked under a tree and everyone fell straight to sleep from exhaustion.

Daylight brought surprises. They had parked in the shade provided by a mighty baobab tree. Robbie was still asleep on the back seat when Jane stepped from the vehicle and looked up at the tree towering eighteen metres over her. She placed her palm over her brow to shield her eyes from the sun, regretting for the first time that she hadn't brought any sunglasses. When her eyes adjusted to the morning light she gasped in amazement.

The landscape gently rolled in front of her to the distant horizon. The wide open, brown and green grasslands contained pockets of dense acacia trees and the occasional towering baobab tree but otherwise it was sweeping savannah, a far cry from the claustrophobic confines of the jungle she had grown used to.

It took several moments for her to see that the

myriad of brown dots across the grassland were animals. As her eyes adjusted to the scale, she realised that what she had assumed were empty plains were filled with wildebeest and zebras – thousands of them stretching to the horizon in a colossal line, all idly grazing in the warm morning light.

It was a truly magical sight that took her breath away. She moved position to get a better look when a noise to her right alarmed her. At first she couldn't see anything – until she craned her neck and realised that three giraffes were grazing on the top leaves of a nearby cluster of acacia trees. She could see their long tongues nimbly pulling the greenery from the spiky branches. Only when they moved did Jane notice several more giraffes feeding from another thicket of trees. Their dark-brown spots allowed them to blend into the landscape with surprising ease. They didn't appear too bothered by her presence.

Robbie woke up with a start. The first thing he saw was a huge set of slender giraffe legs walk past the windscreen.

'Wow! What the . . . ?' Then he joined Jane outside and took a moment to take in the view. He looked around curiously. 'Where's Tarzan?'

Jane felt a creeping panic when they couldn't see him. She was used to him vanishing into the depths of the jungle, but out here she felt vulnerable – there was no place to hide. They stayed by the jeep for the next hour, watching the giraffes gracefully move on to the next cluster of trees.

Robbie examined the GPS, noting that they had made great gains on Rokoff during the night. He appeared to have stopped somewhere ahead. If they pushed on today they might be able to catch him up.

Tarzan eventually appeared from the waist-high grass and Jane felt relieved. There was a mischievous gleam in his eyes, and she suspected he was enjoying exploring his new surroundings.

'Where have you been?'

'No food for Jane,' he said, wiping traces of blood from his mouth. 'Only grass.'

Jane looked away, not wanting to picture Tarzan sinking his teeth into the raw flesh of some hapless animal.

'It's OK, we have plenty of food,' she said pulling a trail-mix energy bar from her pack, one of many given to them by the mechanic Tarzan had threatened to burn alive. 'Rokoff has stopped somewhere ahead. If we move now we stand a good chance of catching him up.'

At the mention of the Russian's name the playfulness left Tarzan's face and he nodded grimly.

They climbed into the jeep and pressed on. The road was nothing more than a dust trail and the suspension creaked alarmingly as the car rocked. Several times they crossed dried stream beds, forcing the four-by-four over some extreme off-roading terrain. Robbie shifted into a low gear and navigated admirably across the wilderness.

Jane lost count of the times they drove close to huge herds of mainly wildebeest, although dozens of zebras walked amongst them with their small foals sporting brown stripes. It surprised Jane when the zebras barked at the passing vehicle; she had expected them to neigh like horses. The occasional ostrich also appeared, watching them from a distance. And at one point Robbie spotted a pride of lions basking on some far-off rocks. He gave them a wide berth, determined not to stray into any unwanted trouble.

Jane was more enthralled with each passing hour. The herds of animals appeared never-ending, and the savannah offered beautiful rolling hills of green and brown in its vast, breathtaking landscape.

Robbie kept an eye on the fuel gauge and judged they had enough to last at least until nightfall.

After a while, at Tarzan's command, Robbie stopped the jeep to allow a herd of some twenty elephants to cut across their path. The savannah elephants were even bigger than Tantor and had huge flapping ears – to help them cool down in the heat of the open plains. Several elephant calves were in the centre of the herd, which prompted one huge female to approach the jeep, ears flaring wide, this time as a sign of aggression. The elephant gave a deep bellow. Her raw power was frightening, and Jane had no doubts that she could easily tear the vehicle apart.

Tarzan however, was undaunted. His eyes gleamed as if he relished the challenge. He opened the door and swung on to the jeep's roof. This only agitated the elephant further and her trunk arced back as she trumpeted furiously.

In return, Tarzan beat his chest and gave a holler that carried far across the savannah. Jane was astonished to see the elephant step backwards and bellow again. Once more Tarzan unleashed his cry and jumped up and down on the roof with such energy that the vehicle rocked and he dented the roof. Then suddenly he stopped and leaned forward, reaching out his hand and grunting softly. The elephant hesitated then cautiously extended its trunk, first sniffing Tarzan's hand and then his head.

The elephant visibly relaxed and gave a gentle snort before it continued walking with the rest of the herd as if nothing had happened. Tarzan offered no explanation and they too carried on. Jane always marvelled at Tarzan's ability to communicate with animals and, for the first time, she wondered where he had learned such knowledge. It couldn't have

been something D'Arnot had taught him. She suspected the answer might be even more mysterious.

As the day wore on, the trail grew more difficult
as the grasslands undulated and became crisscrossed
with deep gullies and dried riverbed. The heat was
making Robbie feel irritable and every sharp jolt
tested his temper as he banged his head against the
side of the door.

Several times they were forced to navigate around
rivers that snaked across their path. Then they would
follow the river, avoiding *duro* and *gimla*, until they
found a suitable place they could safely ford. The first
few times, Robbie drove through the water slowly.

But when it happened again, Robbie wasn't quite
so patient. These detours weren't helping close the
gap between them and Rokoff. He floored the accelerator and the jeep bounced across the river kicking
up a huge curtain of water, that splashed through the
open windows soaking them all.

'You moron!' shouted Jane.

Robbie laughed, but stopped short when the engine stalled on the far side. Luckily it was a gentle
slope up from the river rather than a steep bank, and
the car rolled to a halt. Robbie turned the key and
the engine coughed pathetically.

'Robbie kill it?' asked Tarzan.

'Robbie idiot,' muttered Jane.

Robbie ignored her as he tried the engine again. Nothing. 'I think the carburettor's flooded.'

'Is that bad?' asked Jane, worried they could be stranded in the middle of nowhere.

Robbie didn't reply. He pulled the bonnet catch and climbed out. He lifted the heavy metal bonnet open and stared at the engine. The heat from it was intense and he couldn't touch anything to see where the problem lay.

'We're gonna have to let it cool down,' he said sheepishly.

'Great! Just when we start catching up with Rokoff, you go and do this!' snapped Jane.

Tarzan climbed from the vehicle and scouted the immediate area. The trail ahead cut through thick clusters of trees. Birds flew in the boughs too slender to support Tarzan's weight. Instead he slowly climbed on to a rock, his head twitching left then right, listening to the sounds of the savannah.

Robbie prodded the engine, breathing in sharply through his teeth when he touched the scalding metal. Jane was already feeling too hot just standing next to him and fanned herself with her hand. It did nothing to cool her down.

'Can you fix it?' she asked. Robbie shot her an offended look. He could fix anything. Jane didn't doubt his skills, she was just angry he'd impulsively damaged their ride. 'Why did you drive like that?'

'I'm fed up with being so far behind Rokoff. I wanted to catch up.'

'Well, it hasn't done much good, has it? And we wouldn't be in this situation if you hadn't brought that creep back to the camp,' she reminded him.

Robbie straightened up, ready for an argument. 'Oh, so this is all my fault, is it?'

The incessant heat sapped Jane's patience. She knew she shouldn't wind him up, but she couldn't help herself. 'Yes! If it wasn't for you then Rokoff wouldn't have found Karnath! We wouldn't have been racing through jungle and savannah to save him! We would have been back at the camp relaxing!'

'I thought you hated the camp? What about everything you said about going back home?'

Jane avoided his gaze. The pause was enough for Robbie to turn his back on her and return to the engine. 'You know what? I don't care if you want to go or you want to stay.' He didn't mean it but he was angry. 'I'm only interested in getting enough money to leave this continent as soon as I can. There's nothing here for me.'

Jane noticed he hadn't defended his decision to bring Rokoff to the camp, but she had seen the regret in his eyes as he turned away, and she felt bad for bringing it up. Robbie set to work pulling electrical leads from the engine to dry them with a rag. Jane sat in the jeep to keep out of his way. At least the shade provided some protection from the searing sun.

Everything inside had been thrown to the floor as the vehicle bounced through the river. She started picking things up and tidying them away. Crumpled maps, a collection of rusting tools – socket spanners, screwdrivers, everything needed to repair an engine on the road.

Then she noticed something silver lodged behind the pedals. Removing it, Jane was surprised to see it was a small video camera. She switched it on and looked at the dozen or so thumbnail images on the touchscreen. She tapped the first clip and a shaky image of the jungle appeared; a video clip taken from several metres behind Jane and Tarzan. Jane was shocked – Robbie must have taken it. As if to confirm this, his whispering voice started narrating the scene as if it was a wildlife documentary.

'Here we have the person who calls himself Tarzan, but you will know him better as Lord Greystoke.' The picture zoomed in on Tarzan, but Robbie had shot it as he was walked, so it was difficult to make out any features clearly.

Confused, Jane played the next few clips. They

were all shaky images of Tarzan as he walked ahead – including a rather more impressive shot of him bounding up a tree. As Jane went through the clips, the camerawork improved as Robbie seemed to be taking the videos while stationary. He caught a couple of Tarzan's strong profile, which matched the photographs Jane had seen online of Tarzan's real father. One sequence ended abruptly when Tarzan suddenly looked straight at Robbie and his camera – the image focused on Robbie's boot before it stopped. Robbie's reaction to hide the camera was pointless – after all, Tarzan would have no idea what he was actually doing.

But *why* was he doing it?

The answer came in the very last clip. It looked like Robbie had wedged the camera behind the sun visor as they rode in the car and was asking Tarzan about D'Arnot and the Greystokes. Now Jane realised what Robbie was planning. She stormed from the vehicle just as the engine spluttered to life.

Robbie looked delighted. 'Hey, I got it! The fan belt had just splashed water on the leads.'

Jane was too angry to care about the engine. She thrust the camcorder at him. 'What's this?'

Robbie's smile vanished. 'Where'd you get that?'

'You were videoing him to get proof he's a Greystoke, weren't you?'

'Jane . . .'

'You were going to use this to try and get a reward, right?'

Robbie was immediately on the defensive. 'You were going to do exactly the same thing so don't try and take the moral high ground now!'

'No, I wasn't! I wanted him to decide for himself – and I certainly wasn't doing it for money! Didn't you ever wonder why they never believed D'Arnot? Why nobody ever came looking for the aircraft? Because Tarzan's cousin, William Cecil Clayton, inherited the whole estate – everything! That's why!'

Robbie was confused. 'So?'

'So why would he want to give it all up to the rightful heir? Don't you see? They tried to arrest D'Arnot, and put him under psychiatric assessment so it would look as if he was lying! They don't want Tarzan back!'

'But the reward . . . ?'

'Maybe that makes it easier to find and get rid of him?'

'You don't know any of that for sure! This is just you being overprotective as usual!'

'*Buto!*' Tarzan's warning wasn't heard over their argument.

'I'm not being protective! I'm being sensible—'

'BUTO!' yelled Tarzan as he sprinted towards them.

Robbie and Jane suddenly looked around and saw what was making Tarzan run. A fully-grown rhinoceros was charging straight at them.

Robbie slammed down the engine hood and realised he wouldn't make it safely inside the vehicle from where he was, so instead he slid across the bonnet.

At the same time, Tarzan grabbed Jane and manhandled her though the passenger door. He didn't have time to climb in so slammed it shut, just as Robbie made it over to Tarzan's side.

The jeep acted as a buffer between them and the angry rhino. Its curved horn punctured the mudguard – narrowly missing Jane as she scooted behind the steering wheel. She felt the rhino's hot breath as it snorted and pushed the vehicle sideways through the mud.

'Whoa!' She dodged the tough horn.

Tarzan leaped on the car's roof in a crouch to avoid being crushed.

Robbie wasn't so agile. The edge of the jeep clipped his leg and he slipped over in the mud. He screamed as the jeep slid towards him – then passed over his head! The clearance underneath was just enough to prevent him from being run over – but now it was a matter of seconds before he would be trampled to death by the beast.

Instinctively he grabbed the chassis and clung on for his life as the rhino pushed the vehicle towards the river. The hot exhaust pipe burned his forearm, but he dared not let go.

Tarzan leaped from the roof on to the rhino's neck. He gripped tightly with both hands, unable to reach his knife. He tried sinking his teeth into the beast's leathery flesh, but that did nothing to stop its rampage.

Suddenly, the rhino backed away. With the sound of grinding metal, it withdrew its horn and now spent its energy trying to buck Tarzan off its neck. With nothing to grip on to, he was hurled from the rhino. He rolled in the grass as the beast wheeled around and pawed the earth, ready to trample him.

Inside the car, Jane tried to start the engine but it just wheezed and died. Tarzan might be Lord of the Jungle, but he wasn't indestructible; he couldn't defeat every animal opponent. He still hadn't stood up and Jane doubted he would survive if the rhino charged him. Desperately she honked the jeep's horn and yelled through the open window.

'Hey! Over here! Come on!'

The animal's ears twitched and its head turned, nostrils flaring. It may have had poor eyesight but it had identified its noisy target. The rhino turned from Tarzan and galloped towards Jane.

Realising what she'd done, Jane scrambled for the ignition wires Robbie had twisted together to hotwire the car. They sparked, burning her fingers. Wincing, she had no choice but to reach for the seat-belt and hold on.

Robbie was still underneath the jeep when he saw the animal charge.

'Jane! Get out!'

Too late. The rhino slammed into the side of the vehicle with such force it flipped it over. Robbie held tightly to the chassis as the jeep spun around a full hundred and eighty degrees – then his grip failed and he was flung clear. He sailed through the air to land with a splash in the muddy river.

Inside, Jane had just enough time to click her seat-belt on as the car turned upside down. Then the rhino struck again and its horn smashed through the passenger door. The entire car spun around on its roof, the door ripping off its hinges as the rhino struggled to free itself.

Jane sucked in a lungful of air ready to scream, but the breath was knocked from her as the rhino struck again. It rolled the jeep over completely, back on its wheels and into the river.

The rhino stood on the bank and grunted victoriously. The passenger door was still impaled on its horn, but it didn't seem to notice. It pawed the ground and snorted even louder. Tarzan slowly stood as the rhinoceros turned towards him and charged.

Jane pressed the accelerator and tried the engine again. The jeep suddenly roared to life. Robbie splashed his way through the river towards her and clambered through the space where the passenger door had been.

'Go!' he yelled, waving his hand towards Tarzan.

Water sprayed from all four tyres as the vehicle skidded forwards. They were in the shallower part of the river and Jane hoped that water wouldn't stall the jeep again. Luck stayed with them as they accelerated on to the bank.

Ahead, Tarzan was running for his life. Just as the rhino was about to catch him, he leaped to one side out of its way, nimbly rolled to his feet and sprinted back towards the jeep. The rhino skidded to a halt, kicking up a cloud of dust as it changed direction.

Jane hit the brakes and Tarzan leaped into the vehicle as the rhino lumbered straight towards them.

'Buto angry!' he said.

'Really?' Robbie's tone dripped with sarcasm – something Tarzan didn't understand. 'Reverse!' he yelled at Jane.

Jane mashed through the gears. As the rhino filled

the windscreen she felt the gears bite and hit the accelerator. The jeep lurched backwards, picking up speed. Jane arched around so she could see behind, one hand looped around the passenger seat. There was no way she wanted to go back into that river.

'Faster!' squealed Robbie.

'I've only ever driven forwards before!' she screamed.

The rhino was gaining on them. With its head bowed, the broken door pierced on its horn resembled a battering ram.

Jane pressed the pedal against the floor, and the engine screamed.

'Hold on!' Robbie leaned over and yanked the wheel two-thirds of the way around, making the jeep suddenly spin in a wild U-turn. Stones and dust filled the air as it turned the other way.

'First gear, now!' he yelled.

Jane obeyed, her movements mechanical. She could see nothing out of the window and had to trust Robbie. She put the jeep into gear and they powered forward. Jane laughed triumphantly and glanced at the wing mirror . . . her smile faltering when she saw the persistent rhino racing out of the dust cloud. It quickly caught up with the jeep. Its mighty head butted the side of the car, denting the rear wheel arch and shattering the back window. The vehicle shuddered as it tipped on to two wheels. Jane twisted the steering wheel and they landed back on all four. She crunched her way into second gear and accelerated.

The spurt of speed put distance between them and the rhino, which finally gave up its pursuit. Jane watched in the mirror as it pawed the ground and shook its head – the car door still firmly attached. Then it turned around and disappeared into a thicket of trees.

Jane's fingers hurt as she gripped the wheel. With a clang, the front bumper fell off and they bounced over it without stopping. Tarzan was grinning like a child as he glanced behind.

'Buto!' he said jerking his thumb towards the beast.

'Yeah, Buto,' said Robbie trying to wipe the dirt from his face. 'I don't know what you did to anger it back there, but please . . . don't do it again.'

Despite the extreme danger they had just escaped, Jane couldn't help but laugh as the tension drained away. She also felt relieved that, in the heat of the attack, she had tossed Robbie's camcorder through the door and into the river. That made her laugh even more.

18

A gunshot echoed across the savannah and the wail of an injured elephant carried with it. Rokoff chambered another round and ruthlessly finished the job. As the mighty bull fell dead, his men set on the ivory tusks with chainsaws.

Paulvitch watched, instructing the men on how to cut the ivory. The fight with Tarzan on the boat had rendered his right hand useless and, even though he'd had it set in an improvised cast, without an X-ray he had no idea if the bone was set straight. He feared he would never have the full use of it again.

Rokoff returned to the vehicles. He had hired three trucks and a safari Land Rover to complete his journey, and packed them with supplies, spare parts and a hired a bodyguard team of ten local thugs – he was leaving nothing to chance. The gunshots and chainsaw noises upset the little ape and he could hear Karnath whimpering from behind the canvas of the rear truck. Rokoff had only stopped to kill the bull elephant as it strolled across their path because Paulvitch had insisted on seizing the opportunity. The ivory would make a welcome addition to their fee. Rokoff had killed the elephant almost on auto-pilot. There was no hunt, no moment of elation as he outwitted the animal. His mind was back in the jungle with Tarzan.

The ape-man's abilities were truly incredible. Rokoff had never seen a more perfect example of a human. Every muscle defined, the effortless agility to leap across large distances and the raw strength to take on the fierce boat crew Rokoff had hired – all combined into the perfect predator.

At the best of times, Rokoff treated the people around him with contempt. He was convinced that anyone who wasn't Russian was inferior and claimed that he could trace his own lineage back to the great tsars. He didn't see Tarzan as a person, but as another wild beast, worthy of the hunt.

He broke from of his daydream once the elephant tusks had been loaded. Already vultures were circling overhead and it wouldn't be long before hungry hyenas and other scavengers fed on the carcass.

As the three trucks grumbled to life, Rokoff climbed into the back of the one holding Karnath.

The little ape had been making a din ever since they stopped and it was beginning to grate on his nerves.

'Shut up!' Rokoff kicked the cage in fury, sending Karnath cowering into a corner, whimpering quietly. Satisfied, Rokoff jumped from the truck and took his seat behind the wheel of the Land Rover. The convoy headed across the Tanzanian savannah, towards the Ugandan border.

★

Robbie was unsure which would give out first, the battered jeep or the fuel. The rhino had buckled the rear offside wheel and the entire vehicle shuddered as they bumped across the wide grassy plains. He was relieved not to be driving and was content to navigate Jane around any treacherous obstacles. Her driving had improved immeasurably from when he taught her in the middle of the jungle, especially with no trees around here to crash into.

Suddenly there was an ear-splitting screech from the rear wheel and at the same time the engine spluttered, indicating they had run out of fuel. The car rolled to a halt just as the back tyre bounced in a hole and snapped the axle. It was lucky they hadn't been travelling at speed.

A quick check was all it took for Robbie to confirm the jeep was beyond repair. They would have to walk. They gathered their backpacks from the car and crammed in as many stolen provisions as they could. It was already mid-afternoon and the landscape was so ferociously hot that Robbie could feel his scalp burning. Tarzan bowed his head although the heat didn't seem to bother him much.

'Where are we?' said Jane taking in the savannah and the vast columns of grazing wildebeest that stretched into the distance. The nearest animals were only metres away – she could hear their constant grunting and smell the overriding stench of cattle.

Robbie studied the GPS and adjusted the scale, something he hadn't done for a while. He was shocked to discover Rokoff's tracer was very close. He moved the GPS around from east to west, settling on a straight north-eastern route. From here he could see a small hill, beyond which vultures circled.

'We're close. Very close. Rokoff must have stopped for a while.'

'Where is he?'

'About three kilometres over that hill. From up there we could probably see him.'

'Great! Just as we have to walk!'

Tarzan peered at the hill. 'Rokoff there?'

Robbie nodded. 'If we had the car we would have been on top of him within an hour. But he's moving on again now.'

'Car dead?' said Tarzan prodding the jeep with his bare foot.

'Car dead,' Robbie confirmed, imitating Tarzan. He sighed and leaned on the vehicle. 'And when we get anywhere near Rokoff he'll see us coming.'

Tarzan looked around, studying his surroundings, forming a plan. 'No. Rokoff not see.'

He cupped his hands around his mouth and bellowed. It was a melodious yodelling cry that echoed across the plains. Jane had heard it once before and it filled her with hope.

★

'Sixty-four kilometres,' said Paulvitch as he studied the GPS. 'Then I'm going to a damned hospital.'

'You can wait until we reach Kampala,' said Rokoff quietly.

'That's another two hundred and forty kilometres on a boat!'

Rokoff shrugged, keeping his eyes on the path ahead. This close to delivering the gorilla, he didn't want to risk grounding the convoy in a ditch.

'Then make your way to Mwanza. They have a good hospital there.'

Paulvitch scowled. 'And leave you to claim our pay cheque without me? You must think I was born yesterday, my friend.'

Rokoff smiled. Out in the wild they had no choice but to trust each other, but when it came to financial dealings, Paulvitch needed to touch the money himself before he accepted it was real.

The sun was balanced just over the horizon, casting spectacular rays of light through the clouds. Herds of zebra and wildebeest lined the route ahead, many galloping away, nervous, as the convoy cut through their lines. The collective brays of the animals were louder than the vehicle's engines.

'We won't make it before nightfall,' Rokoff commented.

'I'd rather not camp out here another night, if it's all the same,' said Paulvitch as he rubbed his broken hand. He expected a snide comment from Rokoff, but none was forthcoming. Instead Rokoff kept glancing in the wing mirrors, his brow furrowed.

'What's wrong?' asked Paulvitch.

'I'm not sure.'

Rokoff rolled to a stop and cut the engine. The vehicle's sliding roof was already open to cool the Land Rover down. Rokoff stood on his seat and peered out. The three trucks behind had stopped too. Agitated animals were milling all around them. Behind the convoy, dark storm clouds blotted the horizon and silent sheet lightning pulsed between them. Without the sound of the engines, all Rokoff could hear was the constant murmuring of hundreds of animals running past him. He peered into the distance then fished a pair of binoculars from the back of his seat. He looked out across the herds, but could see nothing but a mass of bodies and dust. Something was not quite right.

Paulvitch joined Rokoff standing in the open sunroof. 'Lions?' he asked. He had witnessed a hungry pride of lions scare a similar-sized herd before. But when big cats attacked, the animals usually only ran out of range before stopping and continuing to graze. These animals just kept running. Then something caught his eye. 'What . . . ? What *is* that?'

Something was moving within the herd. It was heading in their direction. Rokoff raised the binoculars again. His view was obscured by dust – then Tarzan's face suddenly appeared. Rokoff gasped, dropping the binoculars in shock. Tarzan was only two hundred metres away and powering towards them on the back of a zebra. Robbie and Jane followed, also on zebras, clinging to the animals' manes.

Nikolas Rokoff was struck dumb. He had never seen such a sight. The ranks of wildebeest thundered towards the convoy and, within seconds, hundreds of animals were rampaging between the vehicles as plumes of dry dust obscured everything.

The Russians covered their faces with scarves so they could breathe freely. Rokoff finally found his voice. 'Don't let him near the ape!' He grabbed his rifle and jumped off the vehicle – straight into the path of a wildebeest. He was forced to flatten himself against the Land Rover to avoid being trampled.

Then gunshots rang out. Three of his hired lackeys were standing on the tailgate of the nearest truck taking shots at the figures riding towards them. Robbie and Jane, risking falling from their mounts, hurled rocks at the men, their backpacks brimming with more ammunition.

Rokoff ducked as a rock glanced off his head and shattered the Land Rover's side window. He could feel the blood roll down his forehead. The girl had thrown it. He fired at her, but in the chaos and dust it was impossible to take aim. He shouted to the convoy drivers.

'Let's go!'

Rokoff noticed one of his bodyguards had Tarzan in his sights, but before he could pull the trigger there was a flash of yellow and a sleek cheetah leaped from the dust cloud, claws extended. The man cried in pain as the cat cannoned into him and they both fell from the truck. Rokoff heard his screams choke as the cheetah tore into its prey.

The drivers all started their engines at the same

time, concluding that they only stood a chance if they moved.

Jane galloped her zebra across the path of the middle truck, hurling a rock straight through the windscreen. It shattered, striking the driver on the head. The man slumped over the wheel and his heavy foot pressed the accelerator, making the truck lurch towards the one in front.

Jane only just managed to clear the space between them as the two trucks collided. The impact knocked one of the gunmen off the tailgate of the middle truck and he fell under the herd's hooves.

In the cab, the unconscious driver was yanked aside and his passenger took the wheel. The vehicles lumbered forward. Several wildebeest were caught under their wheels, unable to escape.

Rokoff glanced in the Land Rover's mirror – and when he looked up he was almost on top of a zebra. The animal bounded clumsily on to the bonnet, hooves slipping on the smooth metal surface. One leg smashed through the windscreen and broke the headrest of Paulvitch's seat. He had been leaning forward to pull a pistol from the glovebox and narrowly missed being decapitated. The zebra slid across the bonnet and fell to the ground, where it picked itself up, dazed but unharmed. Paulvitch tried to shoot the animal out of spite, but missed.

Behind, Jane and Robbie hurled more rocks at the convoy. Tarzan wheeled his zebra around, his heels digging into the animal's flanks as he urged it towards the last truck. He gained distance on the truck, just as one of Rokoff's hired poachers pulled the canvas sheet away, rifle in hand. He saw Tarzan just metres behind, did a double-take, then brought the gun to his shoulder.

Tarzan sprang up so that he was standing on the zebra's back. For a moment he seemed to be surfing the animal before he propelled himself forward, into the back of the truck.

He landed in front of the gun-wielding bodyguard and gripped the rifle with both hands. Since the thug wasn't about to let go so easily, Tarzan angled the weapon and hit him in the face with the rifle butt. The man was surprised to be struck by the very gun he was holding. Tarzan flipped him over his shoulder and, bouncing off the tailgate, he fell under the thundering hooves of the herd that followed.

Tarzan's gaze swept the truck. There was no sign of Karnath. Six long ivory elephant tusks lay on the floor. They were still flecked with blood. Tarzan felt his pulse quicken as he was gripped by rage. Then he saw another man, crouching in the shadows. The bodyguard sprang forward, a machete in his hand.

The first blow sliced across Tarzan's chest, drawing

blood as it sliced into his flesh. Tarzan barely registered the pain. He caught the man's hand as he slashed again with the blade. Only now did Tarzan notice this new poacher was as big as he was – and he had the upper hand as he pressed his weight down on Tarzan. The blade inched closer to Tarzan's face and both men's muscular arms shook as they wrestled.

The bodyguard then drove his elbow into the bleeding cut across Tarzan's chest. The pain was excruciating and Tarzan felt a moment's weakness buckle his arms. The machete slammed down with the man's full weight behind it.

Tarzan turned his head aside – the blade nicked his ear lobe and ricocheted from the metal floor. With his weight behind it, the bodyguard over balanced and fell sprawling across the truck, clanging against the tailgate.

Tarzan was first to stand as his opponent grabbed the truck's canvas side to pull himself up.

'I'm gonna gut you like an animal,' the man snarled. He tossed the machete into his other hand, menacingly slicing it through the air as he took a step towards Tarzan.

Tarzan picked up one of the heavy ivory tusks, using both hands to wield it like a spear. Then he hurled it with all the force he could muster.

The herd around Rokoff was showing no signs of thinning out. They were moving so fast that the vehicle bounced wildly across the uneven ground. One pothole jerked Rokoff from his seat so violently that he banged his head on the Land Rover's roof.

He glanced in the mirror and was glad to see the trucks were following. Then to his astonishment, he saw one of his men sail from the back of the rear truck – skewered through the chest by an ivory tusk. The screaming man vanished into the dust cloud.

He saw Tarzan climb from the back of the truck and on to the cab roof. Tarzan reached in through the side window and plucked out the driver. The truck veered sharply as it hit a deep rut in the ground, and then flipped like a caber, crashing on to its roof, ivory spilling everywhere – just as Tarzan leaped on the next truck.

'Shoot him!' Rokoff yelled to Paulvitch.

Paulvitch nodded and stood up through the sun-roof, trying to stand firm as the Land Rover swayed around him.

★

Robbie had ridden a horse before, but only once, and he'd never ridden a zebra. He was finding the

whole experience extremely uncomfortable. Nevertheless, he encouraged the zebra alongside the lead
truck and lobbed the last of his rocks through the
window. Both missed the driver. The driver swerved
towards Robbie, almost running into him. As
Robbie tried to steer the zebra away, a pair of strong
hands grabbed his hair and his jacket and he was
dragged into the back of the truck.

★

Jane was distressed to see Robbie disappear into the
truck. She tried to turn her zebra towards him by
pulling its mane, but the truck abruptly veered to
the side, revealing Rokoff's Land Rover just in front.
Paulvitch was bouncing from side to side through the
sunroof when he spotted Jane and took a shot. Luckily, it fell wide. Jane frantically steered her mount in
a zigzag to avoid the shots that followed.

She saw Tarzan throw two men and a supply crate
through the side of the other truck then climb
through the ripped canvas, intent on delivering
punishment to the driver. He obviously hadn't found
Karnath there. Jane realised both Robbie and the
gorilla were on the same truck, the one that had now
slowed to the back of the convoy, probably to con-
fuse them.

From his vantage point on the Land Rover at the

head of the convoy, Paulvitch caught sight of Tarzan clinging to the side of the cab, ready to throttle the driver. The Russian swung his gun at him, unable to aim as the jeep bucked on ruts in the ground. His first shot narrowly missed Tarzan and punctured the truck's radiator. Steam spewed out as he fired again.

Just then a pair of cheetahs drew alongside the Land Rover, their sleek spotted bodies undulating as they easily kept pace with the vehicles. One tried to jump up – its claws raked the rear window but then it fell, tumbling safely away.

The other made a clean bound on to the roof, claws digging into the metal as its fierce jaws bit down on Paulvitch's broken hand, and a claw slashed at his face. He screamed and shot wildly. The cheetah jumped from the Land Rover unharmed, with Paulvitch's plaster cast in its mouth.

Paulvitch's stray shot grazed Tarzan's bicep and hit the driver of the second truck. The entire vehicle lurched sideways, bounced from a rock and rolled through the grass. The herd parted and moved from the path of destruction as pieces of broken metal flew in every direction. The remaining truck, containing Robbie and Karnath, swerved sharply around the wreckage.

'Tarzan!' Jane yelled. There was no sign of him.

The last she'd seen of him, he was clinging to the side of the flipping truck.

She raced towards the wreckage, pulling on the zebra's mane to bring it to a halt, then jumped off and ran over to the scene.

'Tarzan?'

The mangled truck was strewn across the grassland. Smoke poured from the smashed engine. She saw an arm poking from underneath a flap of canvas and pulled the cloth away, revealing Tarzan beneath. He was motionless, his body covered in blood, although she was unsure whose.

'No!' She knelt down, unsure what to do. 'Can you hear me?'

Her stomach knotted and she felt ill. Tarzan couldn't possibly be dead, could he?

She looked up to see the Land Rover and remaining truck heading towards the horizon. On board were Karnath and Robbie. She knew the little ape would be in safe hands – after all there was a collector waiting for him. Who knew what fate awaited Robbie.

The herd dispersed and the pair of cheetahs licked their wounds, taking shelter from the harsh sun under a large acacia, watching her. Jane had no idea what to do. If Tarzan were dead, she too would undoubtedly die out here, alone.

19

Robbie was furious. He felt foolish for allowing himself to be captured and now found himself in close proximity to Nikolas Rokoff. To his surprise, Rokoff had been a perfect gentleman and offered him water and food after saving him from the thugs in the truck beating him black and blue. Rokoff had yelled at them. He even struck one man with a knotted rope until he was bleeding.

'No one is to harm him,' Rokoff growled threateningly.

'What are you going to do with me?' asked Robbie, determined not to show any fear. Rokoff just smiled and said nothing.

They finally stopped at the edge of another huge lake and boarded a motor yacht. Karnath's cage was carefully lifted on board under the Russian's watchful gaze. The journey across the lake took the entire night, but Robbie was too full of adrenalin to sleep.

A quick search of his cabin revealed it was impossible to escape – the windows were too narrow to crawl through and the door was locked.

At dawn they reached a bustling port near the city of Kampala. Rokoff led Robbie to a waiting Land Rover and bundled him in along with Karnath's cage. They sped through the streets without Rokoff saying a word. The city looked much like any other and soon they arrived in the wealthy business district where skyscrapers dominated the city.

They entered an underground garage beneath a large glass tower block, which was filled with luxury cars. Robbie didn't have time to admire them as Rokoff hurried his party to a service elevator.

'What are we doing here?' Robbie asked again. He never received an answer. Rokoff ignored him and the four menacing armed men, who carried Karnath's cage between them, glared at him as they ascended.

They ushered Robbie in to a luxury penthouse apartment, tastelessly decorated throughout with animal skins and mounted heads. Ataro Okeke greeted Rokoff with open arms, kissing him on both cheeks. The Russian was clearly uncomfortable but tolerated the embrace. Okeke crouched to look at Karnath.

The little gorilla was silent, watery brown eyes

staring fearfully back at the man. Everything about the room looked and smelled wrong to the ape.

'Magnificent!' breathed Okeke. 'He's truly magnificent! Nikolas, you have excelled yourself. In fact, since the order was placed I have had several other interested buyers contacting me with better prices. Now we're going to have an auction for this beauty!'

Rokoff smiled. That was typical Okeke, playing one bidder against another. He wasn't the most reliable person to do business with.

Okeke turned to Robbie and studied him carefully. 'And what have we here? Does it have a name?'

'Robert.'

'Robert . . .?' Okeke prompted.

'Just Robert.'

Rokoff remained silent, but smirked as if humoured by Robbie's defiance. Okeke sneered and slowly circled him. 'How mysterious. An American out in the wild, defending a wild gorilla with his own life. How did that happen, Robert?'

Robbie thought of several excuses he could use, but Rokoff cut him off before he could speak.

'He's part of an illegal logging team in the Congo. I used them to get close to this.' He pointed at Karnath. Robbie noticed that he didn't mention Tarzan.

'Illegal logging, eh?' said Okeke to Robbie. 'What

would your embassy think of that if I turned you over?'

'I think they would be more interested in the fact that you're hunting endangered species,' Robbie replied sharply.

Okeke stopped in his tracks and Rokoff gave a low snigger.

'You forget your place. Telling your embassy you are alive would be a mercy compared with killing you and dumping your body out in the savannah. Trust me, no one will find you there. They never do.'

Robbie felt a chill run through him. Okeke's voice never rose in pitch, but the malice in his eyes was unmistakable.

'I've got a feeling he's going to be quite useful yet,' said Rokoff as he moved to the window and gazed across the city.

'How so?' said Okeke, never taking his eyes from Robbie.

'Because there's a private investigator looking for him. There's a bounty on his head.'

Okeke's eyes widened. 'How much?'

Rokoff ignored the question and gazed at Robbie, who was startled by the comment. 'You see, a good hunter knows his prey. I know all about you, Mr Canler.' Robbie reacted in surprise when he heard his name. 'I know what you did. What you're running from. I even left a little trail for the investigator to follow.'

Robbie glowered. He felt nothing but hatred for Rokoff. He was pretty sure that he could overpower Okeke; the man looked like he'd enjoyed one too many luxuries in his life. But there was nothing he could use as a weapon against the Russian. In fact, he didn't think he could beat him no matter what the circumstances were.

'He'll be worth hanging on to for a while,' said Rokoff with a smile.

Robbie was unable to remain silent any longer. The Russian's arrogance needed putting in its place. 'You know that won't be for long. You know who's coming. He won't stop until we are both free.' He nodded to Karnath. 'And he has no mercy.'

Okeke looked between them both, clearly confused. 'Who?'

Robbie ignored him. His gaze remained on Rokoff. 'There is no way of stopping him. You can't reason with him or bargain with him. He will find you.'

To Robbie's surprise, Rokoff started to grin and his eyes narrowed with delight. Then he reached into his pocket and pulled out a small metal disk. He held it up for Robbie to see. It was the GPS tracker Robbie had slipped in there.

'I am counting on it, Mr Canler. I am counting on it.'

★

The twitching vein in Tarzan's neck was the first sign of life Jane saw as she knelt by his side. At first she thought it was a trick of the shadows. Darkness had rapidly descended and there was now a full red moon. It provided some light across the savannah and her torch lit up the area immediately around her. A herd of zebra was still grazing close by and their gentle grunts and squeals gave her some reassurance.

Jane pressed her finger against Tarzan's neck and found his pulse. It felt strong. She swatted flies away as they landed on his chest, knowing they could carry disease. She thought about trying to find water, but had no idea where to look and she didn't think leaving a wounded Tarzan near the cheetahs was wise. She didn't know how far the bond of respect between Tarzan and the wild animals went.

Eventually, Tarzan's eyes flicked open. Under the circumstances, most people would clutch their heads and try to find the strength to stand, but Tarzan stood straight up. When he wobbled slightly, Jane caught his arm until he found his balance.

A pair of spotted hyenas lay in the grass close by, the light reflecting in their eyes. They had been judging Tarzan as a potential meal, but now he growled at them and they fled, gibbering, to join others of their clan feasting on the crushed bodies of the wildebeests run over by the truck.

'Rokoff?' said Tarzan, his mouth almost too dry to get the words out.

'Gone,' said Jane. 'He took Karnath and Robbie with him.'

Tarzan kicked a fragment of the broken truck and stared at the horizon.

'But we still have this.' She pulled the tracker from her backpack. The stationary blip flashed rhythmically.

Tarzan sucked air through his teeth in pain. He usually bore pain in stoic silence, so this reaction alarmed Jane. Pointing to his wounds, she said, 'You need those treated.'

Jane shone the light across his chest and Tarzan inspected the cuts. Only the machete wound across his chest gave him pause for thought. He ripped a strip of canvas from the truck and then examined the twisted engine, pointing to where he wanted Jane to shine her light. Tarzan covered the canvas with oil leaking from the sump and wrapped it around his chest to form a basic bandage.

'No *busso*,' he explained. Jane frowned and Tarzan

pointed to the flies that circled her torch beam. '*Busso.*'

Jane understood: the oil would keep them away.

'If we rest for a bit and leave before dawn we can beat the heat of the day,' Jane began.

Tarzan shook his head. 'No rest. Go now.'

'I don't think you're in a fit state to walk anywhere.'

'No walk.'

Jane shone her torch across the herd of zebra. The light sent murmurs of unrest through it.

'You want to ride another *pacco*?' she said choosing Tarzan's word for zebra.

'No *pacco*. Need to travel fast.' He nudged her torch beam out over the herd and she let out a confused *huh* when she saw his unlikely choice of transport.

The flock of ostriches looked too gawky as they sat close to a hardy shrub, unaware of their new role in Tarzan and Jane's next mission.

★

An hour before the sun crested the horizon, the sky was filled with the eerie shadowless pre-dawn light. Waves lapped the shore of the huge lake that stretched before Tarzan and Jane. They dismounted the ostriches that had carried them through the night at speed, passing nocturnal predators such as a pride of hunting lions, navigating difficult terrain where a four-legged steed would have stumbled. The birds had been tireless and surprisingly easy to control. If it hadn't been for the dire circumstances, Jane would have found the journey quite enjoyable.

Now the lake appeared to be their final hurdle in reaching Karnath and Robbie. After some scouting around, they discovered a small locked hut with several boats moored on a jetty. A sign read: RUBONDO ISLAND NATIONAL PARK, LAKE VICTORIA.

Jane recalled a little of what she knew about the lake from her lessons with Esmée back at the camp. It was one of the largest tropical lakes in the world and sat between Tanzania and Uganda. She wished she'd paid more attention to Esmée. Her lessons had seemed trivial and dull at the time, but now that knowledge would be invaluable.

Since the only way to Karnath was across the lake, after checking that no one was around, they took one of the boats. Jane had no trouble starting the outboard motor and they headed across the calm water.

The journey was long and uncomfortable. Further out, the water became choppy and soon the small boat was being tossed on waves more likely to be found at sea than on a lake. It was clear they had the wrong boat for the voyage but they had no choice other than to press on.

Jane tried to ignore her seasickness. The cool wind and water spray made her feel a little better as she gripped the boat's wheel to keep it on course. After a couple of hours her arms were numb and she felt so exhausted that she had to hand steering duties over to Tarzan.

Hours passed as the storm jostled the boat – several times it keeled far over in the water and Jane was convinced they would flounder, but Tarzan stayed firm at the wheel and kept their course.

After several restless hours the weather calmed and they saw land, which Jane initially mistook for the shore. A chart she found on the boat revealed it to be the island of Kalanga. They navigated around Kalanga and it was almost dark before they saw the lights of the lake's northern shore ahead.

They docked in the small city of Entebbe. Even at night, Jane could see it was a more civilised place than Sango. People were dressed in suits or work clothes and gangs of youths wore grubby trainers. Tarzan looked completely out of place there and it made her even more anxious.

Jane noticed several lorries loading cargo from a ship that had docked. 'We need to hitch a ride into the city,' she said and nodded to a lorry. 'That might take us there.'

The vehicle she pointed to was adorned with faded lettering on the door: 'Kampala Wholesale'. Rokoff had mentioned the city of Kampala before – it was their only lead. The GPS marker was close and hadn't moved so she suspected Kampala wasn't too far off.

She guided Tarzan on to the open flatbed of the lorry just as the driver started his engine. They hid between sacks of grain as the vehicle pulled on to smooth roads. Signs for the airport passed them by, and another one indicated Kampala was only thirty kilometres away. A quick check on the GPS confirmed that they were heading in the right direction.

As they got closer to their destination their surroundings increasingly became manmade. An endless sprawl of tin shacks came into view, stretching into the darkness. Washing hung from lines and stray dogs picked through the rubbish in the street.

'Is this the furthest you've been into a city?' whispered Jane.

Tarzan nodded. 'Furthest Tarzan been from home.'

The shanty town soon gave way to more sturdy cream and orange brick buildings, some stretching ten storeys high. The concrete jungle was becoming denser by the minute and when the lorry pulled up at a large warehouse, the stowaways took the opportunity to slip off the truck. Keeping out of sight, they walked off down one of the main streets.

The solid pavement felt uncomfortable under Tarzan's bare feet and he found the maze of brick and concrete claustrophobic. Power and phone lines hung overhead. Litter blew in the gentle breeze and every shop was heavily shuttered. Signs for mobile phones, pizza restaurants, clothing and alcohol were everywhere they looked. Jane thought they could have easily stepped into any downtrodden street in America. She was thankful they had arrived late when the streets were deserted and they were less likely to draw attention to themselves.

At the end of the street the road climbed gently up towards a cluster of skyscrapers marking the city centre. The GPS was leading them there. Shop signs around them started to change, most bearing the name 'Nakasero Hill', which Jane guessed must be the name of the suburb.

She adjusted the scale of the GPS regularly. It was beginning to look like Rokoff was located in one of the huge tower blocks ahead. One well-lit stone building looked so luxurious and futuristic, with its sloping walls and saucer-shaped roof, that for a second she forgot they were in Africa. The name HILTON was highlighted at the top of the hotel and

Jane suddenly felt pangs of homesickness with the thoughts of warm showers, comfortable beds, and room service . . .

Her daydreaming was cut short by a wolf whistle. Jane snapped back to reality. A gang of teenagers appeared from the shadows, barring her path ahead. She glanced around and saw more had appeared behind her to block her escape. Parked cars to the left hemmed her in. More alarming, there was no sign of Tarzan. Was the big city too much for him? Where had he gone to?

'Looks like someone took a wrong turn,' taunted a large boy with a crooked nose. He looked like a fighter.

'Yeah,' chimed a girl next to him, who had a piercing through her lip. 'This is our street. And you's trespassin'.'

'I'm just going home,' said Jane pointing ahead. 'I don't want any trouble.'

The boy flashed her a menacing grin. 'Well that's tough, ain't it? 'Cos we do. Gi'z your money and passport and that phone too.' He indicated to the GPS.

As Jane slipped the GPS into her pocket, something snapped inside her. She felt a confidence she had never experienced before. Recently she had faced far worse danger than a bunch of bullying kids and she wasn't about to let herself be mugged this close to her destination.

'I suggest you turn around and walk away real fast. No, not walk. *Run*. Run as fast as you can.'

With a chorus of clicks, an assortment of flick knives and butterfly blades appeared in their hands. The gang leader flipped the knife over his fingers and around his palm, but Jane was not intimidated.

'Really? You want to do this?' Her defiance caused murmurs of uncertainty amongst the muggers. They were used to their victims immediately surrendering and cowering in fear. 'Well, come on then. Let's get it over with.'

Jane saw the leader give a quick nod and heard movement behind her. After being in the wild for so long she was surprised to discover her other senses had improved and she anticipated such a simple ambush.

Jane nodded her head backwards and heard a satisfying crack as she struck the boy behind her in the face. She dropped to her knees as he went to grab her again, causing him to trip over. He crashed to the floor and Jane stood on his back, one foot pressing his face into the concrete and shocked herself by screeching wildly like some savage ape.

The teenagers hesitated, then just as their leader raised his knife to strike, Tarzan's feral roar answered

Jane's. The concrete amplified the ferocious cry. The gang looked around frantically, thinking a lion had strolled into town.

Tarzan stood at the top of the three-storey building next to them, poised on the corner and silhouetted by the moon. He howled again and beat his chest before jumping down.

A parked car broke his fall. The roof buckled and the windows shattered, blasting the muggers with safety glass. The vehicle's alarm began to wail as Tarzan went for the leader, grabbing the hand wielding the knife. Bones crunched under Tarzan's vice-like grip. The teenager screamed as Tarzan picked him up and effortlessly threw him through the windscreen of another car.

Most of the gang scattered. They had no intention of facing such a crazy man. Only two stayed to challenge Tarzan. One slashed his knife through the air in a figure-of-eight movement while the other pulled off a heavy chain he had been wearing across his chest and flicked it at him and Jane.

The chain arced over Jane's head, narrowly missing Tarzan as it slammed into a parked car, denting the door. Before the thug could retrieve it, Tarzan grabbed the chain and yanked the boy forwards. He caught him in his crushing embrace. The boy screamed as Tarzan squeezed so tight that bones began to crunch.

'Tarzan! No!' shouted Jane. Tarzan paused, the boy was crying and gasping for breath. 'We don't kill people in the city.' It was all she could think of to prevent bloodshed. 'We have laws.'

Tarzan stared at her for a long moment and Jane began to wonder just how she could make him understand. Then Tarzan dropped the boy to the floor.

'Tarzan is law,' he growled.

The boy limped to safety. Jane and Tarzan looked around and saw the final mugger was still standing there, blade raised, frozen to the spot. Tarzan took one step forward. The teen dropped his knife and fled.

Jane took her foot off the first mugger's head and gave him a nudge with her foot.

'You can go now,' she said lightly.

The boy whimpered and bolted across the street as fast as he could. Tarzan gave Jane a disapproving look.

'Tarzan not like civilisation. Too much danger.'

The sky was getting lighter and, as dawn approached, Jane urged him on. Soon they reached the base of the first skyscraper. Jane slowly swept the area with the scanner until the dot on the screen aligned directly in front of her. She looked up at the twenty-storey apartment block straight ahead. It looked new, gleaming with white stone and glass and the tracker seemed to be stationary up in the penthouse.

'Rokoff's on the top floor. Question is, how do we get inside?'

Tarzan approached the entrance and ran a hand over the smooth walls. Then, to Jane's astonishment, he took a running leap at the wall. His powerful leg kicked off from the smooth surface and propelled him higher. He landed on the narrowest of ledges, his toes hooking to grip as his strong fingers slipped into the flimsiest of gaps between the polished brick-work.

'Come,' said Tarzan, indicating upwards with a nod of his head.

'I'll wait here,' Jane said, knowing she couldn't follow Tarzan up the wall. 'You go in then come back down and open the door for me.'

Tarzan continued his daredevil ascent, using the balconies as springboards to each higher level. Jane thought it was an impossible task without ropes and climbing gear, but Tarzan ascended the smooth structure with grace and ease. Never once did he pause or hesitate. Every action was fluid and natural. In just forty seconds he reached the top floor where he flipped on to the balcony and out of Jane's sight.

★

Robbie flinched as the patio window suddenly imploded and Tarzan rolled into the apartment. Flecks of glass cut his back, but as usual Tarzan didn't react.

'Tarzan!' shouted Robbie, desperate to remind him that they were friends and not enemies. 'They've gone.'

Robbie was bound to a chair by a thick rope. Tarzan tore the ropes away and Robbie rubbed his limbs to restore his circulation.

'Where Karnath?'

'They've taken him. Where's Jane?'

'Jane outside. Where Rokoff go?'

Robbie ran to the video intercom and saw Jane waiting at the doors downstairs. He buzzed her inside. 'To a ranch . . . I don't know where. This place belongs to Ataro Okeke, who ordered the kidnapping. He's preparing to auction Karnath to the highest bidder.'

Tarzan looked around the room, seeing the macabre display of dead animals decorating every surface. Robbie cowered as Tarzan vented his fury. He smashed display cabinets, casting their contents to the ground. He tore pelts from walls, threw the huge plasma-screen television through the window and hurled the leather sofa into a thin partition wall, knocking off several mounted animal heads. The sofa lodged midway through the wall, hanging like a bizarre artwork.

Jane entered during the rampage and watched as Tarzan suddenly calmed when he finally noticed the gorilla's skull that had fallen from a shattered display cabinet. He gently picked it up and ran his fingers over the bone.

'Karnath gone. Tarzan can't find . . . Tarzan fail.'

They had seen Tarzan pass through a range of emotions, but defeat was the most chilling. Jane couldn't bear it.

'But why did the GPS lead us here?'

Robbie showed her the tracking marker that Rokoff had placed in his pocket before he had left. 'He wanted you to find me and not Karnath.' But exactly why had been bothering him. What game was Rokoff playing? It was obvious Robbie would tell Tarzan about the ranch. Was that what Rokoff wanted? With the clock ticking, he didn't have much time to dwell on that.

Jane looked around the room. 'If this apartment belongs to Okeke then there's a good chance we'll find information about his ranch.'

Jane and Robbie began hunting through the cup-boards and drawers, reading every scrap of paper they could find. Tarzan stood on the balcony feeling wretched as he watched the sun rise over Kampala's urban sprawl. Traffic was beginning to clog the streets below and aircraft circled in the distance, their wings catching the sun as they prepared to land at the airport. It was a bleak, alien landscape to him.

'Got it!' Jane suddenly said. 'Look.' She spread out several documents on the floor. One was a map showing the layout and location of the ranch. 'These are the deeds. Okeke owns all of this.' She tapped an address on the page. 'We've got to get there.'

'How?' asked Tarzan.

Robbie grinned. 'When they brought me here, I noticed some very nice cars in the garage.'

20

Rokoff had been on edge since they'd left Kampala and headed the eighty kilometres north-west to Okeke's ranch. The hunter was happy in both the wilderness and the city, but today was different. He knew, without a doubt, that the greatest opponent he had ever met was on his heels and death came with him.

Okeke had been keen to start the auction as soon as possible and sent word to the bidders that they, or their representatives, must be at his ranch by midday. Already the starting price for a young mountain gorilla in perfect condition had climbed to $400,000 as more bidders joined the auction.

The ranch was well away from the prying eyes of the law and approachable only by a long dirt track from the main road. Despite the wide open spaces, Okeke kept the animals he traded in the stables where the small pens restricted their movement and made them easier to handle.

Rokoff placed Karnath's cage in an empty pen, then slowly walked back along the line of miserable-looking prisoners: an okapi, a pair of young giraffes taken when their mother was killed, a juvenile elephant and a highly endangered baby white rhino. Rokoff had trapped most of them. When the animals were first caught they were noisy and aggressive, now they were quiet and passive. The fight had been beaten out of them and replaced with fear.

Rokoff crossed to an open corral outside the large wooden mansion, which was kitted out with the very latest technology; the roof was clad in solar panels and a large satellite dish hung from one end.

Parked outside were several vehicles that had arrived in the early morning; these belonged to private collectors for whom money was no object and obtaining the rare and protected species was a badge of success. Rokoff had no interest in the bidding. Although he hunted for money, cash wasn't important to him. It was just a useful aside to what he enjoyed doing. He looked through the window and studied Okeke entertaining the collectors. Several laptops were open displaying satellite video feeds of other collectors who were unable to make the meeting at such short notice.

He sat down in a swing chair on the porch, his hunting rifle across his lap. He had stripped and cleaned the Saiga with meticulous care, wiping away the moisture from the jungle and the dust from the savannah.

He peered down the winding driveway as a trail of dust rose; the telltale signs of an approaching vehicle. Out here, the flat dusty plains made it impossible to launch a surprise attack. Rokoff's fingers tightened around his rifle as he waited to see who it was.

★

Tracing Okeke's ranch on the map had been pretty straightforward. Jane found several car keys in the apartment and they took a heavy-duty Range Rover from the garage. Within an hour and a half they would reach the ranch but they had no plan on how to tackle Rokoff and Okeke once they were there. This would be the last chance to rescue Karnath and both Robbie and Jane thought a direct assault would prove disastrous.

'We don't have Numa, Sheeta or Tantor here to help this time,' cautioned Jane. 'Rokoff has guns and you know he's not afraid of using them. Even you can't stop a bullet, Tarzan.'

Robbie nodded. 'And who knows what kind of security Okeke will have at the ranch.'

'Tarzan hunt Rokoff to the death,' snarled Tarzan.

Jane sighed. 'If we just run in there and bullets start flying, then what about Karnath? He could get shot. We have to think about this carefully.'

Tarzan stared stubbornly through the window. He was restless and eager to end the hunt.

'There's another thing we should think about,' said Robbie suddenly. 'Rokoff knew I had planted the tracker on him. Why was he letting us follow him?'

'Rokoff like Sabor. Play with prey not kill straight away.' Tarzan indicated to Robbie. 'You still alive because of this.'

'Why would he do that with us?' said Jane.

Robbie shrugged. 'Because he can? People like Rokoff love watching the misery of others. He's just like my stepdad.'

Jane felt uneasy but couldn't pinpoint what bothered her. She knew Rokoff was a ruthless manipulator, but toying with them all this time, almost killing them with every step . . . it didn't make sense.

'We need some heavy muscle,' said Robbie breaking Jane's train of thought. He glanced at Tarzan. 'If you can't get an army, maybe I can.'

Jane frowned. 'What are you talking about?'

Robbie pointed ahead to a building complex off the side of the road: its sign read 'Uganda Wildlife Authority'.

There was a gleam in Robbie's eye. 'Let's hit Rokoff where it hurts.'

★

Rokoff relaxed when he saw a Hummer growl up the driveway and the last bidder climbed out, hurrying into the house. With everyone assembled the auction could now begin. Rokoff watched dispassionately as Okeke's ranch hands led two young giraffes over to a small pen next to the house. The potential buyers could sit in air-conditioned luxury and look at the animals through large floor-to-ceiling windows. Okeke was determined to sell his whole stock today and was keeping Karnath back as the prize exhibit.

Rokoff would get a bonus if the sale exceeded expectations, but he wasn't interested in the auction – from where he sat, he couldn't hear anything inside the house. The hunt was over for him.

The Russian's senses started to tingle. Having spent his whole life hunting, he relied on his instincts for guidance and he'd developed a sharp intuition. The faintest sound, the stillness of the air, the slightest break in the natural rhythm of the landscape around him would set alarm bells ringing in his head. He scanned the dry flat grassland for telltale signs of movement. Grass moving against the wind, birds suddenly taking flight. But nothing stirred. As great a hunter as he was, Rokoff was not foolish enough to ignore the advantages high-tech security systems gave him. He had ensured Okeke's ranch was fitted with the very latest – nothing could get through without him knowing.

He leaned forward in the swing chair, unblinking eyes watching for the subtlest hint that an enemy was approaching. Although he couldn't see it, he sensed something was heading his way.

★

'So why should I believe you?' said Milton Muwanga, chief officer at the Uganda Wildlife Authority.

Robbie and Jane had rehearsed their alibi before entering the UWA, but Jane was having difficulty sounding convincing because she was so exhausted and worrying about Tarzan following through with his part of the plan. Luckily, Robbie was more accustomed to lying.

'We could hear the gorilla in the back of the truck the moment we landed in the dock.' They had told Milton a story of how they were hiking for charity across Tanzania and into Uganda. It wasn't such a far-fetched explanation; people often did it. The details they could provide about life in the savannah added texture to their story, but Milton was still having difficulty believing there was gorilla smuggling going on right under his nose.

'And nobody else heard this racket?'

'Sure, but it looks like we're the only ones to come forward and tell you about it.'

Milton leaned back in his chair and studied them thoughtfully. Then he stood up and paced the room, pointing at a map of Uganda behind him.

'Bwindi is here in the south-west. It borders the Congo. We have mountain gorillas there. Why would anybody cut across Tanzania to smuggle *in* a gorilla?'

'Probably because you protect so well!' said Jane. 'It must have been stolen to order.' She was beginning to think asking for official help had been a mistake. This officer seemed reluctant to spring into action. 'This is happening right now. You're supposed to be protecting animals within your borders, not turning a blind eye! How do you think the Western media will react if they found out you're doing nothing? I bet your own government would also wonder where all their funding was being spent.'

Milton went rigid, bristling with indignation, but to his credit he didn't allow his temper to snap. Instead he took a deep breath and leaned on his desk, staring hard at Jane.

'I run an honest organisation. Africa is a tough place for business, but I allow no corruption here! We do our job with diligence and to the best of our abilities.'

'I didn't mean to imply—' Jane began.

'And you come here without any evidence and expect me to believe such atrocities are taking place on my watch?' Milton slammed his fist on the desk. After everything they had been through, an angry UWA officer didn't scare them much and Jane was pleased to see disappointment on Milton's face. He had hoped to shock them into admitting they'd made the whole thing up. He changed tack. 'If we were to embark on an investigation and it proved to be fraudulent, then I would have no alternative but to contact your embassy and have you thrown out of my country.'

Jane felt Robbie tense at the suggestion, but he kept his cool. His voice was casual and carefree.

'Fine. If you think we're messing around, deport us. But if you want evidence, then I have two lots of proof you can start looking at: an apartment right here in Kampala and a ranch ninety minutes' drive away.' Robbie unfolded a map they had taken from Okeke's apartment and pointed to the location of the ranch. 'Which do you want to check out first?' said Robbie firmly.

Rokoff watched the giraffes being led back to their pens. He could see Okeke shaking the hand of the hugely overweight collector who had just made the purchase.

The okapi was pulled out next. The animal grunted and strained on the rope around its neck. The handlers hit its rump with a stick, hard enough to make it relent, but not enough to leave any mark that could lower the price during the auction.

Rokoff's radio suddenly squawked to life. 'Alarm twenty-six. South-east wire's just been tripped.'

Rokoff's hand shot to the volume control and turned it down. He rose quickly and strode across the dusty drive, stopping short at the tall brown grass that stretched to the rolling hills in the south. He took the safety catch off his rifle and hunched over as he entered the long grass.

Walking on his heels minimised the sounds he made, but he was still far too noisy for his liking. For several hundred metres he pushed through the grass, relying on instinct alone. He knew where the trip-wires were located along the perimeter of the ranch and the south-east sector provided the fewest possible hiding places for a predator to lurk.

Up ahead, something rustled in the scrub. Rokoff

crouched low, only the top of his head visible over the long stalks. Something was moving towards him. He readied his rifle and took aim.

Out here it was a battle of wits. Predator and prey were on equal terms. He could hardly believe his opponent would blunder so blindly into a trap, yet here it was.

The grass parted and Rokoff's finger pressed against the warm steel trigger. Then he paused. A fat warthog trotted through the grass and stopped short of Rokoff as it picked up the hunter's scent. The warthog's comical tail wagged vertically, before it suddenly changed direction and bolted through the grass.

Rokoff felt a pang of annoyance. He must be on edge if he'd allow a stumpy little warthog to catch him out. Then three gunshots sounded from the ranch. Rokoff turned sharply around, no longer concerned about maintaining cover. From this angle, he could see no sign of movement at the mansion. He twisted the volume control on his radio to ask what was happening – and was rewarded with chaotic screams. Then silence.

They were under attack.

★

Milton Muwanga kicked the debris of Okeke's apartment with a well-polished boot. The rare pelts crumpled on the ground and the precious ivory collection was more than enough to convince him their story was true. Still, something bothered him.

'It's like a cyclone blew through here,' he said, looking carefully at Robbie.

'I know. Amazing, huh?'

Milton examined the window. 'I would say the intruder came through there and tore the place apart.'

Robbie made a pretence of looking at the sofa Tarzan had hurled through the wall. 'I think you're right. It must have been somebody incredibly strong to do this. Wish I was that powerful.'

He patted his own arms for emphasis. While Robbie wasn't weak, Milton had to agree there was no way he could have done this damage.

'Now do you believe us?' asked Jane.

Milton was torn. He had fully expected to find nothing amiss in the apartment, but now he looked again at the map Robbie handed him and wondered just what these kids had led him into.

'If you'd like us to go through it all again, fine. But if they're at the ranch selling that gorilla as we speak then your time is running out,' Jane insisted.

Milton nodded. He hated being dictated to by a pushy foreign girl, but she had been right so far. He pulled out his mobile phone and called the UWA office.

'This is Milton. Put me through to the Minister. I need immediate authorisation for a field operation.'

★

Rokoff sprinted towards the mansion. He was as fit as a man half his age, but running in the heat still drained his energy. He broke out of grass to see one of the bidders had been thrown through the glass-viewing window and the okapi was running free.

Inside the house, furniture had been tossed aside and a businessman had his head thrust into a television set, which sparked and popped. Okeke was outside, hiding behind a jeep, his eyes fixed on the house. Rokoff ran to his side.

'What has happened?'

'A wild man! He's tearing the place apart! He's killed two of my customers!'

Rokoff couldn't hide his smile. Tarzan had somehow used the warthog as a distraction so he could get past him. The Russian felt a hint of satisfaction that the ape-man must consider him a worthy opponent.

'Where is he now?' said Rokoff.

Okeke pointed to the house as a skinny Asian man ran out. With a crack, a rope whipped out and coiled around his neck. The man was yanked back into the house. Rokoff heard a roar that he swore could only be the battle cry of a bull ape. The Asian man's screams were swiftly silenced.

Okeke shoved Rokoff in the back. 'Do something!'

Rokoff refrained from rifle-butting his employer to silence him. Instead he stalked to the side of the mansion, keeping behind the parked vehicles as he did so. He was aiming for a door midway along the building when another man was flung through the wall, wood splintering around him. It was one of Okeke's security team.

The Russian slipped through the door as quietly as he could. It took a moment for his eyes to adjust to the gloomy corridor; the only light came from a pair of narrow curtained windows. Floorboards creaked underfoot but the noise was masked by a scream of another unfortunate victim and the crashing of furniture. He raised his rifle, fitting the stock snugly against his shoulder. From this range he wouldn't even have to aim.

Rokoff entered the room expecting Tarzan to be standing amid total carnage. But the room was bare. The hunter froze – he had heard the sounds just seconds earlier . . .

Then the hairs on the back of his neck rose and he turned slowly. Tarzan was suspended over the doorframe. One hand gripped the rafters, his feet firmly planted at an angle on the wall to keep him steady. He had blood on his fingers and across his face. Rokoff didn't want to know what savagery he had committed. One thing was certain – like all seasoned hunters, Tarzan had anticipated his prey's movements.

'Greystoke!' breathed Rokoff. 'We finally meet face-to-face.' Rokoff showed no fear. If this was his time to die, so be it.

But it wasn't.

With murder in his eyes, Tarzan dropped from the rafters at the exact moment that a blast of compressed air catapulted a steel net that wrapped around the wild man mid-flight.

Rokoff stepped aside as Tarzan crashed to the ground. The impact shook everything in the room. He flailed wildly, but the steel net contracted and made movement impossible, even for the mighty jungle warrior.

Tarzan howled with rage. Paulvitch stood in the opposite doorway, holding a bazooka-like device over his shoulder from which the net had been fired. The side of his face sported a deep fresh scar from a cheetah's claw, while his right hand was a stump, bitten off by the same beast. Rokoff gave him a small nod of recognition, then crouched next to Tarzan as the wild man struggled uselessly.

'Got you at last, ape-man.'

'Tarzan kill you!'

Rokoff laughed and shook his head. 'Now, now, don't make promises you are unable to keep. You don't know how long I've been searching for you. The white ape, the wild man – the heir of Greystoke.'

Tarzan snarled and continued struggling.

'And here you are . . . and you're very real. I started to have my doubts,' Rokoff said dreamily. 'I see D'Arnot was telling the truth, after all. He refused to reveal your location so, as instructed, I shot him and left his body for the jungle to hide your secret.'

Rokoff took pleasure at the loathing in Tarzan's eyes. He knew, before the day was out, Tarzan would die and he would have concluded the ultimate hunt.

21

The tungsten and steel net bit into Tarzan's biceps and calves as he struggled to free himself. Rokoff and Paulvitch dragged him from the house and threw him into one of the animal pens. As soon as they entered the enclosure, Karnath went wild, hooting and shaking his cage. Tarzan responded with a series of low grunts that calmed the ape down.

Feeling it was now safe to come out of hiding, Okeke joined them and stared incredulously at Tarzan.

'What is he?'

'Somebody I've been searching for for some time,' said Rokoff. 'He's mine.'

'He killed my clients back there! Dump his body and be done with it.'

Rokoff shot Okeke a foul look. 'I said he's my business. Go back to your little auction. They'll enjoy the experience of being alive all the more after look-ing death in the face – they'll bid twice the price.'

One of Tarzan's victims had just clinched an ex-travagant deal for the giraffes, and that was money Okeke would never see. He glowered at Tarzan be-fore going to salvage what he could from the remain-ing bidders.

Paulvitch leaned over the pen wall as he watched Tarzan struggle.

'I want to kill him.'

'No,' stated Rokoff firmly. 'This one is mine.'

'Look what he did to me!' Paulvitch held up his stump. 'I'm owed revenge!'

After Tarzan had broken the Russian's hand on the boat, Paulvitch consumed painkillers by the fistful to keep the pain at bay. When Tarzan and the anim-als had ambushed their convoy, Paulvitch had made the mistake of using his broken hand to fend off the cheetah; its ferocious jaws had severed his hand clean off.

Rokoff had done his best to stem the blood by ty-ing a tourniquet around Paulvitch's forearm. When they arrived at Lake Victoria, Rokoff had sent his companion on the back of one of the trucks to Mwanza, where he knew a doctor who could treat his injuries, no questions asked.

Rokoff had little sympathy. 'It was your own stupidity. At least your face is an improvement.'

Paulvitch swore in Russian under his breath. Rokoff was feeling too satisfied to let it bother him. He met Tarzan's gaze. The killer instinct was still alive on the wild man's face. Being caught and bound had done nothing but inflame it.

'All my life I've searched the world for creatures that live on the fringes of legend. To hunt something that has been hidden from mankind all this time . . . I consider that an honour. And you, the mythical white ape, the lost heir to a fortune, the wild lord of the jungle . . . you make the deadliest of foes. Finally, an opponent worthy of me. Why did you think I didn't just kill you when I had the chance? On the riverboat I had you in my sights. Across the savannah I could have shot you a hundred times over. Yet you are here, you live only because I decreed it.' Rokoff spoke faster, his pitch rising with passion. 'You live only because I am the better hunter, only because I wanted you to drag yourself here to my territory for our final face-off. You outsmarted me in the jungle, I'll give you that. I hunted you for a long time and the jungle nearly killed me.'

Rokoff leaned against a post and lit a cigarette. The smoke agitated the animals. He deliberately blew it across Tarzan's face.

'I'd heard the rumours of the white ape. Like others, I assumed it was a rare albino. But I could not find it. Then I heard a French soldier, who was presumed dead, had stumbled from the jungle claiming that the white ape was not only real but he was also the nephew of Lord Greystoke, missing after all these years.

'Of course Lord Greystoke was not happy about this, not happy at all. He had no intention of relinquishing the estate, so he set about discrediting your friend, Paul D'Arnot. If D'Arnot's claims proved to be true . . . then you were not to live.'

At the mention of D'Arnot's name, Tarzan stopped struggling. Rokoff blew more smoke across Tarzan, enjoying the moment.

'More importantly, Lord Greystoke needed to see if there was any truth in the Frenchman's ramblings so he hired me to follow him to find out. D'Arnot was driven back to the jungle, hounded by the media who claimed he was only after Greystoke's riches. At least that was the story reported by the media. You see, I knew D'Arnot had discovered the truth. He was a soldier after all, and had connections in military circles. He also discovered that Greystoke had hired me to track and kill the upstart heir to the estate. That's the real reason D'Arnot fled. To warn you that your own family was out to kill you. To warn you that I was coming.'

Rokoff let the statement linger. He was not sure how much of this was getting through to the wild man. He suspected that Tarzan understood a lot more than he was able to vocalise.

'So I set off on D'Arnot's trail. For weeks I followed him before I realised he was leading me in circles. He was far more astute than I gave him credit for. He knew I was pursuing him. Time was running out, I could not stay in the jungle forever so I confronted D'Arnot to find out where you lived.'

'You kill D'Arnot,' Tarzan stated flatly.

Rokoff barked a harsh laugh. 'Not at first. Initially I applied certain techniques to induce pain. Techniques that get most men's tongues wagging, but not his. Your friend endured unbelievable agony to protect you. There is no sport in torture, and I took no pleasure from it so I put a bullet in him to end his suffering and you fell back into legend. At least until your friends decided to contact the Greystokes and tell them they'd found you.'

Rokoff sucked the cigarette in one long inhalation, then stubbed it out on the post, tossing the butt in the dirt.

'So once more the Greystokes called me. For me it was a matter of professional courtesy to finish what

I'd started. I have a reputation to uphold after all. Okeke's job to get your little furry friend here,' he gave Karnath's cage a kick, 'was nothing more than serendipitous timing; the perfect bait to lure you to my turf. After all, I had no desire to let you hide in the jungle again.'

'Rokoff kill Tarzan?'

Rokoff smiled and nodded. 'Rokoff capture Tarzan; Rokoff kill Tarzan. Of course, I'll only do that after I prove to the Greystokes that you really do exist. I think they would prefer to see your execution live. As soon as Okeke sells your little pal I will set up the video link and Tarzan will die.'

★

It took close to an hour for Okeke to persuade the remaining bidders to stay. They insisted on seeing for themselves that their attacker had been subdued and came to view Tarzan in the pen, bound like some muscled freak-show exhibit. Only when they were satisfied that the wild man was no threat did the auction continue.

Rokoff stayed with Tarzan the whole time – he didn't trust Paulvitch not to do something rash the moment his back was turned. The elephant and rhino were led from the pens and Paulvitch accompanied them, announcing upon his return that they had sold for more than Okeke had imagined possible.

The last item was Karnath. Two of Okeke's security men, who bore fresh scars from their encounter with Tarzan, carried the whimpering ape's cage from the outhouse. Tarzan gave a series of low coughs, but said nothing.

'That's the last you'll see of him,' sniggered Rokoff. 'After he's sold they'll ship the lot of them out. Then you're next, my friend.'

Tarzan said nothing. He didn't rise to the bait.

The minutes passed slowly then the security team returned to deliver the animals to their new owners.

'Let's see if your family's ready to see you,' Rokoff said jauntily.

Although usually highly composed, Rokoff found himself gripped by an excitement he had not felt since the early days when he began hunting. Capturing Tarzan was the pinnacle of his career. Executing him was the only way the hunter could truly claim he had beaten his quarry. He had plans to mount the wild man's head next to the silverback and white rhino he had on the walls of his private collection back in Moscow.

Okeke was entertaining his guests with champagne while he waited for their money transfers to be wired to his account. Rokoff kept away from the crowd and sat in the corner using one of the few laptops Tarzan hadn't destroyed to send a message through to the Greystokes to initiate the video-conference. As he waited for a reply, his leg shuffled nervously, a teenage habit he thought he had lost long ago.

'And this is the man who made everything possible,' Okeke suddenly said. Rokoff looked up as Okeke waved an arm towards him and beckoned him to stand. All eyes fell on Rokoff, gleaming with respect and curiosity. 'Nikolas Rokoff, undoubtedly the world's greatest hunter!'

Okeke initiated a round of applause and the champagne in his hand spilled everywhere. He was elated from the sales, which, in spite of the earlier mayhem, had gone better than expected. Karnath had sold for $800,000 to a wiry German – an agent for a wealthy sheikh.

The applause surprised Rokoff and he found himself suddenly fielding a barrage of questions about how he had managed to capture so many exotic creatures and avoid the authorities. No sooner had he finished one story than the eager audience asked for more details and a glass of champagne was thrust into his hand. Rokoff didn't notice Paulvitch slowly back out of the room.

★

Paulvitch was a coward who thrived on petty feuds and picking fights with the weak. Although he would never admit it, Paulvitch was quite happy lurking in Rokoff's shadow. But that was before Tarzan's beasts had scarred him for life.

Paulvitch didn't share Rokoff's desire to execute Tarzan for the viewing pleasure of the Greystokes. He was impatient and believed showing them a dead body would achieve the same result, but Rokoff was hearing none of it. Paulvitch was too cowardly to kill the ape-man himself, but now that Rokoff was distracted he hurried back to Tarzan with the intention of inflicting serious pain on him. If Rokoff wanted to make the final kill, fine – Paulvitch intended to push Tarzan to the point where he would be pleading for death.

Tarzan looked up as Paulvitch entered. As soon as he saw the wild man, he was consumed with resentment. He drew his hunting knife and pressed it against Tarzan's throat.

'Look at what you did to me!' he snarled, his self-control vanishing. 'Look at my face! I should kill you right now!'

Tarzan lifted his neck, exposing his veins as a clear taunt to the Russian.

'You don't think I'll do it, do you? Like him, you think I'm weak!'

Paulvitch's anger blotted out any common sense he possessed and he began pacing back and forth, never taking his eyes off the ape-man while he ranted.

Although his movements were restricted, Tarzan was still able to move his legs and body. No knife could slice through the steel mesh binding him, but the bottom of the net, around his ankles, was tied with nylon climbing rope – something that a sharp blade could easily cut through.

Paulvitch moved close, spittle flying as he spoke. 'I'm stronger than you, monkey-man! I'm going to make you scream my name!'

He crouched and pressed the knife to Tarzan's throat once again. The move put Paulvitch off balance. He had only the stump to support him but it hurt to put pressure on it.

It was the opportunity Tarzan was looking for. Ignoring the knife, he headbutted Paulvitch in the face. The Russian howled as his nose broke and he reeled against the wall.

'Aargh! That's enough! You'll die by my hand!'

Paulvitch lunged forward as Tarzan spun around and raised his legs to defend himself. Paulvitch anticipated the attack and slashed the knife in a series of uncoordinated blows. The first bounced from the wire mesh around Tarzan's legs. The second sliced through the rope and stabbed his calf. Tarzan registered the pain with a gruff snort — then kicked Paulvitch with all the strength he could muster.

Paulvitch smashed through two wooden pens before crashing against the wall. His back throbbed in pain, but he clambered upright now determined to slay the wild man there and then.

Tarzan stood and pulled the wire netting off his body. Paulvitch saw the ragged nylon rope at the base of the net and realised his mistake. The Russian charged forward with a scream, hoping to reach the wild man before he could fully free himself.

★

Rokoff's keen hearing picked up the faint shrill scream over the noise of the conversation. His gaze swept the room.

'Paulvitch!'

Rokoff pushed past a red-faced American bidder with whom he had been sharing hunting anecdotes and powered to the stables as fast as he could. He took several steps into the building then froze. Paulvitch was swinging from the rafters, the metal net that caught Tarzan now a noose around his neck. His eyes bulged, his tongue was swollen; he had died a painful death.

There was no sign of Tarzan. Rokoff suddenly realised his only defence was the small pistol in his jacket. He drew it and spun round, shooting into the dark corner behind him.

There was no Tarzan.

He swept the gun to the rafters – the ape-man was not there. A dull thumping noise caught his attention outside and slowly he backed into the daylight. Standing away from the building, with plenty of space around him, he felt a lot safer than he had moments ago. The animals near the vehicles were becoming restless; the noise was scaring them. Rokoff shielded his eyes and peered into the sky. He tracked the noise and saw a pair of helicopters swoop low over the plains towards the ranch. Rokoff was certain they were not part of Okeke's plan. He ran towards the mansion, taking cover by the pens.

Okeke and the bidders stepped outside to see what the noise was, just as the choppers banked around the ranch. They were Bell UH-1 Hueys, sporting Uganda Wildlife Authority logos.

Everybody panicked as they realised the trouble they were in. One Huey hovered over the compound, the rotor's downdraught creating a cloud of dust that sent the caged animals into a frenzy. Rokoff saw the side door slide open and he recognised Milton Muwanga from the UWA's frequent press statements, sitting half out with an automatic rifle aimed on the crowd. Next to him sat Jane and Robbie, pointing at Rokoff.

Milton's voice boomed over a loudspeaker. 'This is Uganda Wildlife Authority. On the ground! You are under arrest!'

A second Huey landed a hundred metres away and armed UWA security filed out, rifles raised. Everybody dropped to their knees, including Rokoff. He cursed his decision to keep Robbie alive, but he had needed the boy as bait to lead Tarzan the final steps to the ranch rather than rely on the GPS tracker alone. Knowing Robbie's past he had assumed he would never turn to the authorities for help. A costly mistake.

As the security team moved in, Rokoff calculated his escape route. There was no way he would allow himself to be caught. He fell backwards and swung his leg out, breaking the lock on the elephant's cage. The young elephant immediately bolted. Scrambling to his feet, he did the same with the rhino cage and it too raced for freedom. The young animals caused a stir among both the surrendering men and the rangers. Dust from the rotors added to the confusion and gave Rokoff the chance he needed to open Karnath's cage and pull out the shrieking ape. The little gorilla was almost as strong as Rokoff. He bared his fangs and bit deep into the Russian's arm.

Rokoff shrieked as Karnath drew blood, but he continued to hold Karnath close and ran for the house.

In the helicopter, Milton took aim at Rokoff – he had a perfect shot – but he hesitated when Rokoff turned and used the ape as a shield.

Rokoff carried the struggling gorilla inside. Then he took off his jacket and threw it over Karnath's head. The trick seemed to subdue the ape a little and he started to whimper. Quickly, Rokoff found one of Okeke's tranquilliser guns and shot a dart into Karnath's back.

Outside, Milton's Huey landed and the troops piled out. Robbie and Jane followed, keeping well behind. Unsmiling rangers already surrounded Okeke and his men.

Rokoff knew he only had seconds to make his escape. He shoved the tranquiliser gun in his belt, grabbed his hunting rifle and picked up the drowsy ape. The dart contained just enough sedative for Okeke to subdue any animal that might become too frisky for his clients while still keeping it awake.

Using Karnath as a shield, Rokoff held out his rifle with his free arm. He smashed through a window at the back of the house just as Milton led the raid through the front door.

Rokoff ran for the first chopper that had landed.

The rangers were two hundred metres off to the side, surrounding Okeke's group, so he had a clear run to it.

Behind, Milton's team had stormed through the house, following Rokoff's trail through the rooms and back out the rear doors.

'Stop!' Milton shouted from behind.

Rokoff half turned and bounded sideways towards the helicopter, while firing at the same time. The rifle's powerful recoil almost kicked the weapon from his hand. As he was unable to aim, it was nothing more than a warning shot, but it had the desired effect, forcing Milton and the UWA rangers to hit the deck. With the gorilla in the way, they didn't dare return fire.

The pilot hadn't seen Rokoff approaching from his blind spot just behind him to the right. As soon as he saw movement he reached for a pistol stowed under his seat – but he was too slow and a second later Rokoff was pointing the rifle menacingly at him. The pilot raised his hands, moving slowly so as not to alarm the Russian.

'I can't fly this thing if you shoot me,' said the pilot as bravely as he could.

Rokoff threw Karnath into the back of the Huey then pulled the tranquiliser gun and shot the pilot in the chest.

'I'm afraid you're not needed,' purred Rokoff, booting the man out of the helicopter.

Milton stood and sprinted for the chopper just as the Russian throttled the engine and the aircraft rose from the ground. Several rangers opened fire, bullets pinging from the fuselage.

'NO!' screamed Jane.

'Hold your fire!' shouted Milton. 'The gorilla's on board!'

The helicopter wobbled as Rokoff fought the controls. It had been a while since he had piloted one, but it soon came back to him. The nose dipped and the Huey shot forward – so low that everybody was forced to hit the ground.

At the controls, Rokoff laughed as everybody ducked out of his path. Then he saw movement from the ranch. Tarzan swung from a top-floor window and somersaulted on to the hot solar panels on the roof. He sprinted along the angled panels as the chopper flew alongside.

Rokoff pulled on the collective, making the aircraft rise. Tarzan's intentions were clear – but leaping aboard would be impossible, so Rokoff thought.

Tarzan jumped from the rooftop without any fear of the spinning rotor blades while everyone watched in horror, expecting him to be shredded.

But Tarzan had no such anxieties. For him, this

was no different from navigating through the tree-tops. He soared under the rotors and caught the landing ski with both hands. Momentum sent him under the fuselage and as he swung back he flexed his arms and flipped through the open slide door, into the cabin.

Rokoff was searching the ground to see where Tarzan had fallen. The thrashing rotors masked any sound from inside the cabin as Tarzan picked up Karnath and held him tight. The little ape's arms had just enough strength to hold on.

Rokoff caught the movement out of the corner of his eye. He turned in the pilot seat, inadvertently leaning on the stick and banking the aircraft to the left.

'That's impossible!' he screamed, his words almost lost in the roar of the engine.

Tarzan didn't have time to talk. He just wanted justice. As the helicopter sharply angled under him, Tarzan punched Rokoff so hard across the face that teeth flew out and bounced against the canopy. Rokoff fell against the stick, sending the chopper into a nosedive.

Revenge would have to wait. Tarzan's priority was to get Karnath to safety. He stood at the doorway and braced himself with one hand, holding Karnath in the crook of his other arm. The ground was rapidly catching up.

★

Jane saw Tarzan jump from the Huey seconds before it completed its uncontrolled arc and ploughed into the middle of the mansion. Dust obscured Tarzan and her gaze was drawn towards the devastation as the roof collapsed, solar panels shattering. The Huey's rotors severed and the aircraft tipped on to its side.

Jane braced herself for a huge explosion, but instead a massive cloud of debris shrouded the scene and the smell of fuel grew stronger.

'Run!' shouted Robbie, grabbing her hand and sprinting from the building.

Then the leaked aviation fuel set alight, ignited by sparking electrical wires exposed within the mansion. The helicopter blew apart and the explosion struck the middle of the house like a wrecking ball, effortlessly demolishing walls and floors.

Okeke watched in despair as his mansion was torn in two, but then he was forced to duck for cover as burning wreckage fell around him.

'Tarzan!' Robbie screamed.

★

Robbie and Jane stayed with Milton for an hour. The

fire had spread through the building and razed it to the ground with surprising speed, spitting fat black ashes across the plains. Okeke and his clients were handcuffed and taken to UWA trucks when they arrived on the scene. The caged animals were taken to a vet and a team of rangers went looking for the stray elephant and rhino. Milton assured Jane that they would be humanely caught and safely relocated.

An immediate search of the wreckage revealed no sign of Rokoff, Karnath or Tarzan. Robbie and Jane had watched silently, dreading what they might find. The lack of bodies confused Milton who swore that nobody could have escaped the disaster and got past his men.

He sheepishly approached Robbie and Jane as they sat on the tailgate of a truck. He gazed around, almost unwilling to look them in the eye.

'I suppose I owe you an apology for not believing you, eh?'

Jane shrugged. 'You did in the end. That's what counts.'

Milton nodded then finally looked at them with an embarrassed smile. He offered his hand. 'Congratulations. You broke a major international smuggling ring.'

Robbie winced as Milton crunched his hand. 'I think you should take all the glory for this one.'

Milton smiled; he wouldn't say no to being branded the hero of the hour. 'If you insist, but I will still need your details to contact you so we can follow up the investigations.'

Robbie hesitated, but Jane smoothly chipped in. 'No problem. We're staying at the Hilton in Nakasero Hill. We'll be there for another two weeks. Ask for me, Mary Winter.' She had no idea where the pseudonym came from but there was no way she was going to use her real name.

Robbie had a flash of inspiration. 'And I'm Robbie Canler, from New York.'

Milton nodded as he wrote the names in a small notebook he kept in his breast pocket. He didn't see the shocked look Jane gave Robbie.

When Milton was taken aside to process Okeke and the others, Robbie steered Jane towards one of the bidder's jeeps. The keys were in the ignition, and they took it, slipping away without anybody noticing.

Jane gave directions from a map she found in the glovebox. They were soon bouncing along a rough track and eventually stopped at a crossroads, parking in the shade of a lone acacia tree sixteen kilometres from the ranch. This was the predetermined meeting spot they had arranged with Tarzan: an easy decision, as it was the only landmark for miles. Jane only hoped nothing had gone wrong and he could make it.

Minutes blurred, and Jane estimated an hour had passed before the long grass suddenly moved and Tarzan stepped out with a wide grin, Karnath knuckle-walking along by his side. The tranquilliser had worn off by now and the little ape jumped into Jane's arms. He was more cautious about Robbie, but encouraged by Tarzan, the young ape soon allowed Robbie to stroke his greasy fur.

When Jane told Tarzan that Rokoff had disappeared in the crash, Tarzan just studied the landscape thoughtfully. Nothing further needed to be said.

★

Without the constant pressure of pursuing Rokoff, the journey home was a little more leisurely. Tarzan had an impressive sense of direction in retracing their steps, this time driving around Lake Victoria and across Tanzania. They were able to refuel the jeep using a credit card Robbie had taken from Okeke's apartment.

After a day, Robbie used his satellite phone to call Clark.

'Robbie? Where the heck are ya?' There was no enquiry as to their well-being, just straight to business.

Robbie didn't feel like filling him in on their adventure. That could wait. 'We've been travelling. We're about a week away. Tell Archie that Jane's fine.'

'Yeah, yeah. Listen, some great news about the Greystokes—'

Robbie cut him off. 'Whatever. It can wait until I'm back. I gotta go.' He disconnected as Clark started to protest. He was tired of Clark's scheming and was in no mood to hear what he had to say. He turned the phone off for good measure.

The ferry journey across Lake Tanganyika was uneventful as they hitched aboard a cargo ship that didn't ask any questions about the young ape with them. The crew kept away, wary of Karnath and frightened by Tarzan.

Robbie was keen to avoid any conflicts so they crossed into the Democratic Republic of Congo using narrow off-road trails that were beyond the reaches of frontier guards and drove almost continuously. He and Jane took turns at the wheel and when he wasn't resting he played a little with Karnath and enjoyed talking to Tarzan.

The road soon petered out and they were forced to abandon the vehicle so they could continue on foot through the jungle. Entering the solitude of the rainforest seemed like a homecoming to them all. Jane was glad to leave the dry savannah behind and revelled in the heavy tropical rain as it washed the dirt away.

Tarzan made the trek easier by summoning Tantor and a pair of jungle elephants to carry them home. In the comfort of the jungle, Tarzan relayed Rokoff's confession about D'Arnot. It was difficult as Tarzan still lacked the vocabulary to explain every detail, but they soon built a dark picture of the Greystokes as a family who would kill to preserve their wealth.

Karnath's homecoming was greeted with grunts and hoots of delight from the gorillas, now back at the crashed aircraft. Even the normally aggressive Kerchak was pleased to see Tarzan's return. Karnath's adopted mother held the little ape tight, then began grooming his fur to remove the stench of his ordeal.

Jane was touched by the care and family spirit the gorillas showed Karnath. She glanced at Robbie and saw that he was affected by it too. She had been apprehensive about bringing him here, as she still hadn't forgiven him for secretly videoing Tarzan. But without the camera he could do no harm. She was certain he wouldn't be able to find his own way here from Karibu Mji.

Robbie kept a wary distance from the apes, but they appeared to welcome him – after all, they had met before when they had helped rescue him from Tafari's clutches.

The aircraft fascinated Robbie, but he didn't ask any questions or inflame Jane's suspicions by taking anything away. He could hardly believe he was finally here. But instead of experiencing elation that he finally had the proof he and Clark needed, he felt unusually subdued. Circumstance had brought him and Tarzan together as friends who had risked their lives together and now he wasn't so sure he wanted to do anything to betray him. However, that didn't solve Robbie's problems and he was painfully aware that he still had to fend for himself.

'Family need new home for a time,' said Tarzan watching as the apes lavished Karnath with attention.

'You'll take them towards the volcano?' asked Jane.

Tarzan nodded. 'First Tarzan take you home.'

Jane didn't feel the need to ask if she would see Tarzan again. A bond had formed between the three of them during their adventure and, in a strange way, Tarzan had accepted her and Robbie into his family.

★

Back at the camp, Archie welcomed Jane home with a huge hug. He shook Robbie's shoulder, glad to see him.

'You smell terrible, mate,' he said laughing. 'Where the heck have you been?'

'You really don't want to know,' Jane replied. And

286

she meant it. Her father worried enough and he didn't need to know they'd travelled across half the continent over the last two weeks.

Clark slapped Robbie on the back and made sure Jane wasn't within earshot.

'Good news. That private eye I mentioned was askin' questions about ya. He turned up at Sango then suddenly got word you were in Uganda and left pronto.'

Robbie smiled to himself. He knew Milton's report would raise a few alarms when his name was mentioned and had hoped that would draw attention away from the Congo.

'You get the footage?' whispered Clark.

'I lost the camera,' said Robbie.

Clark looked disappointed, but nodded. 'Still, we got the GPS coordinates, ain't we?' Robbie nodded. Clark's eyes narrowed and he stared at him. 'You've been there, haven't you? You've seen the plane?'

Robbie nodded, but couldn't meet Clark's gaze. He was feeling guilty for betraying Tarzan. Clark smiled and squeezed his shoulder.

'So it's all true. Perfect!' He shouted across at Archie. 'Hey, Arch! Tell 'em the good news.'

Jane looked expectantly at her dad. 'What good news?'

'That,' said Archie pointing over to the bar as

Esmée came out with a tall dark-haired man who flashed a disarming smile.

Jane didn't need to ask who it was. The family resemblance was clear. Her blood ran cold.

The man extended his hand. 'Ah, you must be Jane. A delight to meet you, I've heard so much about your exploits. Allow me to introduce myself. My name is William Cecil Clayton. I believe you know my cousin?'